Praise for

THE CROOKED SWAN

"*The Crooked Swan* is a touching, spellbinding, magical tale that you will not easily forget!"

— David Farland

New York Times Bestselling Fantasy Author

"An engaging story, told with sensitivity and warmth. Plot and characters sparkle with life, and the ending is full of magic. Young adult readers as well as lovers of music and ballet will find much to enjoy in *The Crooked Swan*."

— Dorothy M. Keddington

Author of *The Fairy Thorn* & *Aisling of Eire*

"*The Crooked Swan* is a masterpiece with a depth that brought tears, chuckles, and thoughtful moments; I read it in one sitting. Couldn't put it down! The surprise ending was heartfelt — a pure joy. I can't wait to share it with my friends, children, AND grandchildren!"

— Lynne Thompson,

Author, BYU Ballet Teacher, Owner Academy of Ballet Studios

"I appreciate the beautiful analogy of *The Crooked Swan*; and what a perfect title for your book. It is a great reminder to all of us to love, appreciate, and encourage those we meet in all walks of life who may be challenged in some way. I sincerely love this sweet story. Thank you again for sharing your wonderful book with me."

—Tresa Anderson

Dance Teacher, Owner Charisma Studio

THE CROOKED SWAN

 JULIE HELM

DIAMOND GATE PUBLISHING

Published by Diamond Gate Publishing

www.diamondgatepublishing.com

ISBN: 978-0-578-05851-1

Cover and Illustration Artist: Margaret Lee

Share

THE CROOKED SWAN

with others.

www.thecrookedswan.com

Ask for it at your favorite bookstore.

To my mother
who loved to dance,
and who loved to watch
me dance,
and who now dances, no
longer impaired,
in heaven.

Acknowledgements

I would like to offer a heartfelt thanks to those special people, you know who you are, for helping *The Crooked Swan* become not just a beloved family treasure but a legacy to be shared by one and all for years and years to come.

For all those who helped bring this story to life–a patient husband, children, grandchildren, sisters, other family members, and close friends–thank you. Hats off to Margaret Lee, who captured the essence of the story with her beautiful cover and illustrations and gave it wings to fly. Each has contributed in their very own unique way.

I first wrote *The Crooked Swan* approximately twenty-five years ago. However, raising six children became a priority for several years, and I wasn't able to pursue publishing it until recently. But it wasn't forgotten.

Deciding to publish the story didn't happen by accident. It happened because all six of my children begged me to do it — they believed in the story enough to want me to share it with everyone. How great is that? My daughter, Rebecca, spent hours reading it over with me to get it just the way we wanted. My son, Brandt, wrote a song for it called *The Dancer*. The rest of my children, Amber, Jessica, Trevor, and Jared, offered even more suggestions. Last but not least, my husband, Greg, the love of my life, lent me his ears and advice many times. *The Crooked Swan* has undoubtedly become a family affair.

It's my sincere hope that every family in America reads this story. It's not a Christmas story per say; it's a story that happened during the Thanksgiving and Christmas holidays that affects a remarkable change for good within the hearts of those involved. It can be read any time of the year and still be appreciated and enjoyed.

The Crooked Swan is my gift to you...because don't we all need to be reminded of how wonderful it can be to fulfill our dreams, in spite of the odds?

THE CROOKED SWAN

JULIE HELM

Julie Helm

One

*H*ome sweet home...my mother was talking behind me, but I wasn't listening. Boy, did this ever bring back memories. Buried pain is like a geyser waiting to erupt, I decided, and found myself thinking back to a time when I was sixteen...when my family went on a summer vacation to West Yellowstone to see Old Faithful blow. The boiling hot water shot out of the volcanic earth with such force that it left my mom, my dad, and me breathless. That's how I felt right now...like my emotions were getting ready to spew out of me with enough force it would leave my mother and me breathless, but not in a good way.

"Kayla! Are you listening to me?" My mother's voice cut into my thoughts. "It wouldn't hurt for you to come home more. You have your career, but you also have family obliga—"

"Isn't that why you sent me to ballet school?" I interrupted. "Why you spent so much of your precious money?" Unable to keep silent any longer, I whirled around to face her, allowing the anger and pain inside of me to break free. "I'm a professional dancer. I thought that's what you always wanted?"

"Because I thought that's what *you* wanted!" my mother answered, hands on hips.

Shaking my head, I gave her a bitter laugh. "It's impossible to please you! I'm home for the holidays. Leave it at that!" I sat down on our living room couch and reached for the magazine lying on the coffee table.

"I still want to talk," said my mother, folding her arms across her chest like she was taking a last stand. Add a mustache and curly blonde hair and she'd look like General Custer. "Please!"

"Talk about what, Mom? Because this isn't really about family obligations, is it? It's about her…"

"There are things we need to talk about, and yes, her, too. It wouldn't hurt to give Sophie a call." I knew it. Her voice changed from argumentative to pleading. "She wants to see you. It's been four years since you two—"

"I don't want to call her," I interrupted again. "No! I won't call her, and that's final!" I snapped the magazine open, feigning interest in an article titled "Female Bigfoot Spotted Near Mt. Saint Helens." Some things never changed, I thought, rolling my eyes. As I turned the pages, a picture of Sophie Hepworth formed in my mind—tall, small-boned, and long, wavy auburn hair kissed with natural highlights that put Pantene Pro-V models to shame. She'd been one of my closest friends for years…but not anymore, not since her betrayal.

I heard my mother sigh noisily and knew she was doing it on purpose. She wanted me to look at her. But that wasn't going to happen. "I don't understand you anymore," she said when I finally glanced her way.

I shut the magazine and threw it on the table. Mom jumped a little. I reached up and began massaging my scalp momentarily. "Since when do you understand me? Every time I come home we fight!"

"You're being unfair. All I want is what's best for you. You're my daughter. I love you."

Groaning with exasperation, I stood up. "This is why I don't come home more, Mom," I said in a voice that was louder than I wanted it to be. I didn't want to fight with my mother. I loved my mother, but she could be so darned pushy...and I really hated it when she pushed me. I turned and left her standing in the middle of the living room. As I climbed the stairs that led to my bedroom, I heard her following me.

"Is it really asking too much to give up a little time for your friends and family? You've changed, you know," she said from behind me.

Would it be mean if I packed my bags and left, I wondered? No, I couldn't do that to her or Dad, so I turned and faced her. "Don't you get it? Dancing isn't just a part of me, it's my entire life! It always has been, and it always will be. You saw to that." After all, I had been dancing since I was four years old, and since the age of twelve had spent five weeks out of every year at The School of American Ballet in New York City, in their Summer Intensive Program. Two hundred students were chosen annually to train from across the country, and Sophie and I had been two of those lucky students for five years.

My mother frowned. "That isn't true. Why would you say that?"

"Because you can't have your cake and eat it too! Quit trying to get me to include others in my life when there's no room. It takes an unbelievable commitment to be a dancer."

"I know that!"

I shook my head. "No, you don't. Or you wouldn't call and ask me to write to our relatives. You wouldn't ask me when I was getting married. You wouldn't tell me you longed for grandchildren. You wouldn't tell me how much I've changed. Mom, dancing, for me, comes before family, holidays, children, men... everything."

"Even before life-long friends?"

She was referring to Sophie again. "I've only been home for a couple of hours and you're pushing me, just like you always do, to get your way."

"Kayla dear —"

I covered my ears. "Stop it! Our little talk is over, Mom." I tried to smile but couldn't, so I walked into my bedroom and slammed the door, hoping she would take the hint and leave me alone.

Hands behind my head, I was lying on my bed trying to cool off, staring blankly at a couple of my old teenage rock posters, when I heard the doorbell ring. Let my mother get it.

Moments later, I heard voices, nothing I could make out. A knock on my bedroom door got my full attention. As it squeaked open, Sophie's head poked around the corner. "Hi, Kayla," she said, giving me a slow, hesitant smile. "Is it okay if I come in?"

No. It wasn't okay if she came in. I sat up and threw my feet over the side of the bed. *Mom is going to pay for this one,* I decided. *I might even pack up my bags and leave tonight.* "Why not?" I told her, unable to hide the agitation in my voice. Sophie and my mother probably had this all planned the minute I told Mom I was coming home for the holidays, and I wouldn't be dancing in the Christmas ballet this year. Every dancer needed a rest. Was it too much to hope for while home?

Sophie tentatively came in and shut the door behind her.

"Sophie," I replied stiffly, and then felt myself

softening; it really was good to see her…until the old anger resurfaced. We met in the middle of my room. I held out my hand, but Sophie ignored it with a brush of her hand. Instead, she grabbed my shoulders and gave me a hug, holding me close before letting go. Feeling awkward, I put my hands on her elbows but didn't really hug her back.

I stepped out of Sophie's embrace and let out a startled gasp. She had a bulge on the front of her the size of a watermelon. "Not another one!" I sputtered.

She nodded. "Isn't it obvious?"

Part of me wanted to smile at her, offer her congratulations. Another part of me held back. "You're so big!" I heard myself say instead.

Sophie looked down at herself and back at me. "And as usual, you're too skinny."

I pulled a face that told her I knew she was right. "Lots of hard work these days," I said and looked away, feeling even more uncomfortable. No one knew more than I did how much Sophie had dreamed of becoming a professional dancer and receiving a position with the New York City Ballet, one of the leading ballet companies worldwide. In junior high we had shared each other's dreams, promised, like young ambitious teens do, to help keep each other on the right track. "Just like those first few months in New York." I looked back at her. "You remember those days, don't you, Sophie?"

"Kayla..."

Swallowing hard, I shook my head. Sophie studied me, looking far more concerned than I wanted her to be. "It's okay, I gave up the past four years ago," she said and squeezed my hand.

Anger stirred. "You didn't give up anything until that country boy got you pregnant!"

Sophie clenched her jaw, hesitated, then seemed to calm down. "That country boy stole my heart!"

"You mean you got caught and your punishment was marriage. There are ways of getting rid of unwanted pregnancies."

Sophie placed a protective hand on her stomach. "No one forced me to do what I did. I wanted that baby as much as I want this one."

Some things never changed, I thought again bitterly. "You deserted me! Our dream–"

"You made it without me!"

"Because I resolved after your wedding never to let anything, especially another human being, get in the way of my career. I wasn't going to watch my hopes and dreams ruined, not like yours had been."

Sophie frowned. "My life began when I married David. My dreams weren't ruined. I found myself."

Yeah, right. "I've landed one of the lead roles for a new ballet—my third in two years. I'll be doing everything we always dreamed of doing. Rehearsals start in February. You don't miss that?" There...I'd finally said something that would make her jealous. I hated doing it, but I wanted her to admit she'd been wrong. I wanted her to miss what she had given up—me, mainly—and forgotten promises.

Before I could pull away, Sophie reached out and squeezed my hand. "Your mother told me the other day about the ballet. I think it's wonderful for you, but not for me. I've opened my own dance studio. I'm teaching these days."

She didn't look jealous or sad. She appeared happy for me...now that was a surprise. But why hadn't my mother told me about Sophie teaching? She certainly told me everything else. "Where?" I managed to ask.

"Here in Stansbury."

"Teaching who?"

"Well...I teach children mostly between the ages of four to eighteen. I have about seventy students. I hope to have more next fall."

Sophie stood in front of me, pregnant and looking like it hurt to move, and talking about more students? That seemed ambitious, even for her. "Why children?" I said trying to take in what I had just heard and clamping down on the old hurt and bitterness.

"Why not? We were kids once, you know." Sophie laughed at me then, but it was a forced laugh, like she was nervous and trying to seem more at ease; she was making an incredible effort to bring back the camaraderie of a broken friendship. What was she doing here? "Don't look so repulsed. Somebody's got to teach them, somebody who loves them, Kayla. It isn't every young dancer who can leave home to attend a dance academy of their choice."

"You did," I needlessly reminded her.

"And so did you," said Sophie.

Frustrated, I turned away from her, running shaky hands through my brown hair. I didn't know what to say. The thought that Sophie had changed from an ambitious young woman seeking fame and fortune to a contented mother who actually enjoyed teaching other people's children to dance baffled me. "How can a dairy farmer's wife afford to build a dance studio?" I finally asked.

"We didn't build a studio. I rented part of an old building downtown and remodeled it with our savings. David was a wonderful sport about it. It's been great for me, exactly what I needed."

I turned back to her. "What about the baby? I mean…it's so stupid! You almost died having the last one." The round bulge on the front of her suddenly moved to one side, like it overheard me and responded by kicking its mother. Staring at Sophie's stomach, I noticed it kept moving, stretching one way and then another. "Does that hurt?" I couldn't help asking.

Sophie followed my gaze then placed a hand over the relentless kicker and began making soft gentle circles. The kicking stopped, but she kept rubbing. "Sometimes," she answered. "I get really uncomfortable, but that's because I'm so far along. My feet hurt more than my stomach right now." She walked to my bed and sat down, letting her breath out in a whoosh. "Believe it or not, we planned for this baby. It's also one of the reasons I've come to talk to you. I've wanted to see you for ages, but was afraid you hadn't forgiven me."

So she did know that I was angry, even though I'd never come out and said it; still if I were honest, my actions had probably condemned me. "You talk about forgiveness? I faced New York alone because you broke your promise!"

"Kayla, I want to be friends again."

The hopeful expression she wore on her face was making me feel things I wasn't certain I wanted to feel. "It wouldn't be the same. You have your own little family now; you don't NEED me. Things have changed…you've changed."

Sophie nodded. "That's true to a certain point. But we all change some time. You won't always be a young, skinny dancer. I'm happy with who I am. Please, can't we be friends?" She held out her hands, beckoning, expecting me to kneel down and place them in hers, I supposed. What I really wanted, at that moment, was for Sophie to walk out of my room and not come back. But I knew she wouldn't leave until I answered her. "Okay! We're friends," I said abruptly, ignoring her hands, knowing I sounded as insincere as I felt.

Sophie slowly dropped her hands and gave me a sad smile, still friendly, but more subdued; I could see she was disappointed. She crossed swollen feet and leaned on her hands, which made her stomach protrude even more. "Your mother told me you weren't planning to leave until after Christmas. The baby is due in five weeks, but my gynecologist wants me to get off my feet now; he wants me to go to bed and stay there. He says if I don't rest what happened with the last pregnancy could happen again. Your mother mentioned you might be able to help me out for a while. I thought it would be a great—"

"Me!" I uttered in astonishment.

Sophie gave me a hopeful nod, one that only she could give.

"Doing what?" I said, beginning to feel hot and dizzy every time I took a breath. This was insane…

Sophie seemed uneasy; like she had a secret she wanted to tell but didn't know how to go about it. Her gaze shifted to the wall-mounted shelves where most of my old ballet awards sat collecting dust; her face seemed to fill with fond memories, and then she turned back to me. "Why teaching classical ballet, of course. The Christmas recital is coming up. Most of the kids know their dances. They just need plenty of practice."

That took a lot of nerve to say, especially considering our circumstances, past and present. Frustrated, I backed away from Sophie and turned to my door. This was not happening...not to me. Reaching out a shaky hand, I grabbed onto the knob—a life preserver that would take me to safer waters—and twisted. I could walk out the door right now and let my nosy mother handle this, and Sophie would have to find someone else to fill her shoes. "You're the one who loves children, not me. I don't want to teach a bunch of snotty-nosed brats to dance," I finally said and opened the door. Getting ready to make my grand exit I tried to leave, but my feet betrayed me and wouldn't budge.

Sophie grunted as she slid off of my bed, and I knew that she was walking toward me, that she wanted me to look at her when she spoke because she'd always been sincere like that. She used to have the ability to look into my eyes and make me squirm. But not anymore, I told myself.

"Why not? You've never given it a try. Teaching children can be very rewarding. It has been for me. There's a certain satisfaction in it that's hard to put into words. All I know is the more I teach, the more I like it."

Ears ringing, I turned to Sophie in disbelief. Did she really think there was a chance I'd say yes? After she and my mother had manipulated this whole 'getting reacquainted' thing?

"Well?" she said, and I heard the desperation in her voice.

I took a deep breath. "As your FRIEND," I began, making certain I overemphasized the word, "I think it only fair to be perfectly honest."

Sophie pursed her mouth and nodded. "Isn't that what we've been doing?" She stared into my eyes with uncertainty.

My mother and I were going to have another serious talk after Sophie left today. "I've worked too hard and long to start teaching children," I told her. "I didn't sleep with a farmer and get myself pregnant, trading my career for a family and a herd of dairy cows."

Sophie's mouth parted. "I take it the answer is no," she said in a hurt voice.

Inwardly, I cringed. "You take it right," I said and held up my hands and shrugged.

"I see…." She sighed loudly; much like my mother did when she thought I was making a big mistake. "You know, you would have loved the place. David insisted that everything be first-rate. For now…

it's not overcrowded; it's well lit. My mirrors are fabulous. The floors are solid wood. I have a great sound system. I knew it was a lot to ask, but I don't trust anyone else. The recital is scheduled for the eighteenth of December. I really do need you. You're sure—"

"I'm sure," I said before she could say anything more. "Come on. I'll walk you to your car."

She placed her hand on my arm and gave me a couple of I-feel-sorry-for-you pats. "There's no need. I know the way out. Good-bye, Kayla."

"Good-bye, Sophie." I watched her walk out of my room. When I heard her talking to my mother, I shut my door and retreated to my bed.

My mother barged into my room shortly after I listened to Sophie's car drive off. "Kayla! You've got to be kidding!"

Was it only moments ago I'd wanted to strangle this woman? I looked away from the pain and anger I saw fuming across her face. "I don't want another fight, Mom. I came home to rest," I told her in a subdued voice.

She walked over to the bed, placed her hands on her hips, and hovered over me. "But surely—"

"I don't want to do it. Okay? Please get out and leave me alone!"

She left without saying another word.

Feeling satisfied, yet flustered, I closed my eyes.

The next thing I knew, keys jangled in my ears. My mother stepped into my bedroom, her coat on and wearing a panicked expression.

"What is it?" I asked her quickly and sat up.

"It's Sophie," she said, voice quivering. "Her water broke. Her parents called and said she's in trouble. Grab your coat, I'll take you to the hospital."

Two

$\mathcal{F}$or a lady in her fifties, my mother was a fast driver. We practically flew down the streets of Stansbury and were riding the elevator up to Sophie's hospital room a short while later. Knocking on her door, I found myself ushered inside and standing next to the birthing bed, watching her helplessly. Sophie lay on her back, her bare feet mounted like prize trophies in metal stirrups. She was wearing a blue and white checked hospital gown, crying out in pain and thrashing her head back and forth. The bottom half of her was covered with white linen. Bright lights were shining down on us that were too hot to be comfortable. "Sophie," I managed to say. I stepped closer and saw that her cheeks were stained with tears. Her eyes were bloodshot, and her brow covered in sweat. A man in green scrubs and wearing a blue surgical mask, who I quickly realized was the doctor, sat in a chair at the bottom of the bed. His arms were moving under the linen covering.

David, and a stocky nurse that looked a lot like a younger version of my mother, stood on the other side of Sophie. David was holding Sophie's hand. The nurse held the linen cloth out of the way for the doctor.

"We can't wait for the next contraction. You need to push!" said the doctor to Sophie.

Sophie moaned in pain. "I can't! I'm too tired," she cried.

I glanced at David. He looked terrified.

"Push," said the doctor, more forcibly, "or you and your baby will die!"

Sophie took a big breath and pushed, holding her breath as she did so. The veins bulged in her neck, and her face reddened with strain. She took another breath and tried to keep pushing, but she lost what she'd inhaled in a whoosh of air. "I can't, something's wrong!" she screamed and thrashed her head yet again.

My heart slammed into the back of my throat. I grabbed her hand and squeezed. "Sophie, please, you heard the doctor, PUSH!" I begged.

She turned and noticed me for the first time. "Kayla, why didn't you help me?" She began sobbing. "I needed you!"

Stunned, I dropped her hand, unable to answer her agonizing question.

"This wouldn't be happening if you had..." She stopped speaking, grabbed her stomach, and screamed like she was being torn into pieces.

"Sophie! Again!" The doctor's voice broke through the haze that surrounded us.

I reached for her hand, but she was using it to grip the railing on the bed.

Looking at David the doctor said, "There is too much blood, more than I would like to see." You could tell by looking into the doctor's eyes that something wasn't right. He briskly started giving orders to the extra nurses that came rushing into the room. "Increase the drip; I need forceps and more gauze. Get me an Oxytocin injection to stop this bleeding." Moments passed, and the stocky nurse came in holding a syringe and inserted a clear medicine into Sophie's IV.

Sophie stopped screaming suddenly and gasped, all color draining from her face. As her eyes rolled back, and her head lolled to one side, she lost consciousness.

"Sophie! No!" yelled David.

A nurse quickly readjusted the pads stuck to Sophie's stomach, then watched the electronic machine that was monitoring the baby's heart rate… the small beating heart seemed too slow, far too sporadic. An oxygen mask was placed over Sophie's nose and mouth. "We're losing them," the doctor said anxiously. I stepped out of their way, catching my toe on the metal apparatus that held Sophie's IV bag and nearly tipped it over. It wobbled precariously from side to side. Every person in the room turned to stare at me. Shaking my head in denial, I backed up against the wall. This wasn't my fault.

David turned to me, tears streaming down his cheeks. "Why wouldn't you help?"

I woke in a cold sweat and realized that I'd been dreaming. The sun had set. Early shadows of night filtered through my room. Sitting up, I wrapped my arms around myself and began to rock back and forth on my bed. My chest ached; I was breathing like I'd just run the hundred-yard dash in high school. If my heart didn't quit pounding like a jackhammer, I'd have a heart attack. My stomach was empty, and it was probably a good thing, as I felt like throwing up. Staring out my window at the rising moon, I did something I hadn't done in four years — I cried.

After a quiet dinner early that evening with my parents, my mother being especially not talkative, I borrowed Dad's car and began driving the silent streets of Stansbury, which were coated in a thin layer of freshly fallen snow — seemingly premature for this time of year. I meandered for thirty minutes before stopping at a Maverick and making my way inside the store. A male cashier stood behind the counter reading a magazine. He didn't look any older than eighteen. "Can I borrow a phone book?" I asked.

He didn't say anything. Instead he reached into a cubbyhole under the cash register, grabbed a beat up book, edges tattered, and handed it to me. I quickly looked up Sophie's address, wrote it down on the back of an old receipt I found crumpled in my purse, then thanked the cashier and handed him back the book.

Fifteen minutes later, after double-checking the address, I parked alongside the country road in front of a small red brick rambler. As I opened the car door, a blast of frigid air took my breath away, and had me scrambling back inside my car to grab my leather coat. I glanced to the west side of the home where a couple of black and white cows, yellow tags in their ears, were busy eating patches of dead grass that stuck up through the snow. They raised their heads and stared at me. Further back sat a large gray barn surrounded by skiffs of snow-covered fields. One of the more curious cows that had been staring at me walked toward the pasture fence separating me from it, and mooed. That was the cue, I guessed, for the other cows to stop eating momentarily and moo at me, too. I guess if one cow mooed they all mooed. Dairy cows…it smelled horrible. The stench of urinating animals and overripe manure permeated the air, and I fought against the desire to plug my nose. Was this kind of farming really a job men chose to do? Before losing my courage, I walked up the front sidewalk, and shivering, rang the doorbell.

David answered the door on the second ring, surprise written across his cherubic face. He wasn't tall. I would guess about five foot nine inches; his sandy blonde hair hung shaggy around his ears. He was wearing a faded red and green flannel shirt tucked into a blue pair of overalls. Hand him a pitch fork and straw hat, and I couldn't help thinking he'd look great on the front cover of the *Farmer's Gazette*... their Christmas edition. He hadn't changed much in appearance over the past four years.

My hands made tight fists that I quickly hid in my coat pockets. "I need to talk to Sophie," was all I managed to say. He studied me a moment then turned and walked back into the house without saying a word, leaving the door ajar and me standing outside. I had no doubt that Sophie had recapped our entire conversation earlier that afternoon, as he didn't act particularly friendly toward me. No matter. I didn't need to go into their house to say what I was going to say.

"I'll do it," I told Sophie immediately after she opened the door wide enough to stand in front of me. "How hard can it be to teach your dancers anyway?"

A smile spread across her face like melting butter. She grabbed me and gave me a hug, shoving the basketball she carried on the front of her into my stomach.

"Thank you...thank you...thank you," she whispered close to my ear.

"You're welcome." I hugged her back as emotions shifted inside of me, and I felt a much-needed smile of my own touch my face.

David stepped up to the door and stood behind Sophie. She turned and grabbed his hand. "She's changed her mind. She's going to help me."

Relief washed over him, and it became a 'smiling moment' for all of us again. Sophie hugged us both, drew us against her as tight as she could. I didn't know how I felt about that one, especially since David smelled like the cows out in his pasture, but I went along with it.

"You'll never know how much this means to her," he told me. "Thank you."

"It means a lot to me, too," I said and realized that I really meant what I said. It felt good to smile and hug Sophie again.

Julie Helm

Three

Sophie insisted on driving to the studio right then to give me a tour of her place. "Classes are held five days a week between the hours of four and eight. Two of the intermediate classes come twice a week. Your Saturdays and Sundays will be free for you to do anything you like," she told me while we stood in the middle of her dance floor.

She then spent the rest of the evening and into the early morning hours teaching me the various Christmas dances, including three solos she'd choreographed for her intermediate classes. I took notes in a beat up notebook she gave me that listed the dances with their steps, and marveled at how gracefully she could still move while being pregnant.

"Aren't you supposed to be on bed rest?" I asked her once, yawning.

"Yes, and I will be starting next week, after I make sure you don't need me." That sent a jolt of reality through me. I'd be on my own at the studio...with roughly seventy amateur dancers. Was it too late to change my mind?

"I haven't told my intermediate students, yet,

who will be dancing the solos. If it's not too much bother, I'd like you to help me make that decision," she told me when we were finished dancing and putting our shoes back on. "Take a day or two to get comfortable with the routines, get to know the girls, and then you decide."

We put on our coats. As Sophie dug the keys out of her purse and walked over to the switch to flip off the lights, I was tempted to tell her just how much of a bother she had been already, but I remembered my Sophie dream and kept silent. "Wait, I'd like the names of the intermediate girls you might have in mind for the solos. This way I'll be able to compare my notes with yours," I told her. Sophie recited the girls from memory. I wrote them down in the notebook. Out a small window in the foyer, flakes of snow twinkled through the cold air like tiny dancing fairies. Sophie locked the front studio door. I tucked the notebook under my coat to keep it dry, and as we turned and walked to her car, she said, "You sure you understand everything?"

No, I wasn't certain about anything, except that I wanted Sophie and her baby to remain in good health. "I'll be fine," I told her with more confidence than I felt.

"If you have any problems, you can call me, or don't hesitate to ask my secretary, Jan Stevens. She works at the studio the first hour of each day." She wagged her finger at me playfully. "You aren't getting ready to 'walk the plank,' Kayla, so don't look so terrified. They're just children, not a frenzy of man-eating sharks. Try to have fun with it."

On the first Monday, a little over two weeks before the Thanksgiving holiday, I arrived at the studio to take over the dance classes. In the small room that served as the front foyer, I stepped out of a holey pair of tennis shoes, took off my jeans, and pulled a loose fitting navy sweatshirt off over my head. Standing in a pair of nude tights and a black leotard, I pulled out a pair of well-used ballet slippers and slipped them on, then quickly stuffed the clothes in my bag. There appeared to be hooks for adults and children, and I hung my bag on a taller hook positioned above a long bench near the entrance.

Two hours later I collapsed against the wall that separated the dance floor and the foyer, near Jan Steven's desk. "What class is next?"

"Intermediate," Jan informed me, giving me a sympathetic look. "Most of the girls have been taking dance since they were four. It should be easier than the last two classes." I hated being so transparent, but I was exhausted.

I nodded. "I appreciate you staying longer today. I didn't realize teaching children to dance would be so —"

"Difficult?" Jan finished for me.

"Challenging," I told her.

Jan nodded like she understood completely. "Did you get Alice to the bathroom in time?"

I glanced at my hands and shuddered. "Not entirely. She wet all over me before I could get her leotard down. Luckily she saved the messiest part for the toilet." I hesitated. "Does Darren make a habit of breaking wind in class? He kept doing it every time he did a plié. The rest of the class couldn't quit laughing. He was a nightmare!"

Jan frowned. "He's one of our newer students. I think it's his way of trying to make friends. Sophie warned him last week not to do it anymore. I'll call his mother tomorrow."

I gave her a quick nod then focused my attention on several young girls running through the foyer that I supposed were all part of my next class, as I hadn't taught any of them earlier that day that I could remember. They looked to be between the ages of nine and ten. One giggling little redhead wasn't even aware she had stepped on my toes as she tore past my legs. It wasn't hard to figure out this group wasn't going to be much better than the last. "You can do it!" an inner voice reassured me. "You were a kid once, too."

"Maybe fifty billion years ago!" I screamed back

at my inner voice.

Jan noticed me staring at them. "By the way, your next class is all girls," she informed me, not quite hiding the grin that slid across her face.

"Oh joy!" Grabbing the wood stick I had christened at home in my father's workshop that morning as my dance stick, I walked onto the smoothly polished dance floor. To my left was the fully mirrored wall that ran the length of the room, and I admitted to myself that Sophie had truly spared no expense. Before I could turn away, I caught my reflection looking back at me. I looked as nervous and tired as I felt. The bun I had twisted to perfection in my bathroom that morning had loosened and sat lopsided on my head. As I swallowed, I concentrated on what I was supposed to be doing, forcing the fear to the back of my mind. "Girls," I said loudly and firmly, and I beat the floor repeatedly with my stick. "Take your places at the barre. Quickly!"

The laughing and running around continued as five or six of the little girls gave me measuring looks, and I could see the sooner they learned I was no push-over, the better.

As I continued to pound my stick, I looked down into the sad, blue eyes of a little girl standing next to me. She was watching me, her pale, soft-featured face turned upward. She seemed to be waiting quietly for a turn to speak.

She was dressed in a bright pink, oversized leotard and baggy tights that bunched up in a mass of wrinkles at her ankles and knees. I couldn't help noticing that she was slightly underweight; yet her cheeks were high and full, like a chipmunk carrying a load of nuts. Her hair had been brushed back and put in a tight ponytail. A pink bow that matched her outfit had been clipped in her blonde hair.

The first thought that entered my mind was that this girl would never make a dancer. In fact, I couldn't help wondering why Sophie had placed her in one of her intermediate classes. She looked more like the class clown.

I looked away from her and shouted, "Girls! I mean it! Class has started!" I quit pounding the stick when all the girls, except the skinny girl with the ponytail, had taken a place at the barre. "What is it?" I then looked down at her and asked.

"My name is Narissa Serveen. I'm new. I haven't got a place at the barre."

"You mean," I paused, "you just started dancing?" Narissa had been put in the wrong class. That was easy enough to fix.

She shook her head.

"She's danced here for a while," volunteered the redhead who had stepped on my toes earlier. "She just means she's new in our class."

"My sister says that when Narissa was in her class, Miss Sophie had her stand near the front so she didn't trip on anyone," said another girl, her black hair and porcelain skin giving her the refined appearance of a miniature ballerina figurine, stiff and perfect.

"She's kind of clumsy," said another brunette with frizzy curls that needed a good brushing, and wearing a bright purple leotard...was that a mustard stain on the front of her?

Some of the girls in class laughed at this last remark.

Narissa dropped her head and stared at the floor. A situation like this was exactly why I didn't want to teach children to dance, I reminded myself.

I looked at the young dancers. The blonde with the bun was pulling a face at Narissa while the other girls laughed at her antics. A protective urge flared inside of me. "My mother always taught me it wasn't nice to make fun of people."

"Oh, we're not making fun," said the blonde. "Narissa already knows she's clumsy." She pulled a goofy face and glanced at Narissa. "Don't ya, Nissa?"

More girls laughed.

Thinking it had been longer than I realized since I was a little girl, I watched Narissa raise her head, glance at the girls poking fun, and then nod.

I immediately reached for Narissa's face, afraid that she might drop her head again, and said loud enough for everyone to hear, "My name is Kayla Davis." I looked at each of the girls. "I'm going to be your new teacher until Miss Sophie has had her baby and is feeling up to teaching again. In MY class, we're going to have a motto: if you can't say something nice, then don't say anything at all. That includes pulling funny faces and laughing at others. Do you all understand?" I glared at the girls, waiting for their response.

The girls looked at each other and at me, nodding their heads; they appeared compliant enough...but that meant nothing considering the first half of my day had been riddled with surprises.

"That's exactly what Miss Sophie says sometimes," said another little blonde in pigtails.

"Good!" I said, not realizing until that moment that I had wrapped my arm around Narissa's shoulders; I promptly released her. "That's because Miss Sophie's a professional dancer and an excellent teacher, and she knows better."

I grabbed Narissa by the elbow and began walking her toward the middle of the barre. Each step she took seemed awkward, almost like she was limping. Not wanting to draw any more attention to her than I already had, I chose not to look at her feet. Instead, I asked the two girls who stood in front of us to make a place for her in the middle. "Stay there until I tell you otherwise," I told her when she had stepped between the two girls. I turned and walked back to the front of the dance floor. "Now, if no one has to go to the bathroom," I began, hitting the floor twice with my stick for my own self-confidence more than anything else, "I think we better get a few things straight. Rule number one: From now on, no one talks out of turn. If you have to say something, raise your hand then make certain you address me properly. My name is Miss Kayla. Rule number two…"

I continued to recite some rules I thought necessary for the class, rules I remembered having when I was their age and taking dance. When I was through, I had each girl tell me her name, including Narissa. I didn't want her to feel left out.

The preliminaries over, I started warming up their bodies, using an age-old series of dance exercises. Yet for some reason I was at a loss to explain, I didn't look at Narissa. I knew that I was purposefully avoiding her.

Next I took the class through a series of arm movements that were supposed to be in perfect synchronization with their leg and feet movements. Unfortunately, I couldn't even imagine beginners looking less coordinated, let alone intermediate dancers. As I stopped to demonstrate the five basic feet positions in ballet, I explained to them about the importance of having beautiful arms and hands accompany those positions. Coordination and timing were part of the package too. I knew the information I was giving them was repetitive, something they had heard from Sophie many times before, as all dance teachers said these things, so I couldn't resist the temptation to show off. I did a few leaps, a gorgeous arabesque, and three perfect pirouettes, using my arms with beautiful, graceful precision. The girls squealed with glee and clapped in excitement. Compelled to leave a lasting impression on these young dancers, I asked them all to stand on one side of the room. I swiftly walked out into the foyer, unzipped my bag, and grabbed a CD that I had brought with me. At the bottom of my bag was a white tutu bottom that I'd stuffed in there this morning, and I hurriedly pulled it on over my black leotard. Call me vain, but I love that tutu.

I could hear the girls talking quietly among themselves. I walked back into the room and over to where the stereo sat, took the CD out of the plastic case and put it into the player. I then turned and faced the girls. "Last winter I had the privilege of dancing for the American Ballet Theatre in New York. I portrayed the lead role of Odette and Odile in *Swan Lake*. Would you like to see some of it?"

All of the girls started talking at once, jumping up and down like human pogo sticks. "What's *Swan Lake*? Who's Odette? Oh, yes!" they shouted simultaneously.

I smiled at their enthusiasm. "The part I will be showing you takes place during Act 4 of the ballet. The prince confesses his love to Odile, Von Rothbart's daughter, thinking that she is Odette. In horror,

Odette flees back to the lake and joins the rest of the swan maidens in sadness."

The girls looked enraptured when I finished setting up the scene for them. I pressed the play button and then made my way out to the center of the floor. As the haunting music floated across the room I let it take me, and I have to admit I felt good for the first time that day. As I danced, the girls made perfect little round-eyed owls. I moved fluidly, perfectly, feeling the music as I danced. Tension as thick as maple syrup rolled from me, and I knew that I lived and breathed my part to the very last step of my performance.

"And that's how it's done," I told them when I had finished, and then I removed my tutu and the CD from the stereo and set it on top of my bag. "So let's get busy."

Starting at the front of the barre while taking the girls through another exercise sequence, I began correcting the arms and legs of the individual dancers, keeping the beat with my stick. The redhead, whose hands looked more like she was trying to catch rain than dance, was first. "Let the movement of the arms be an extension of the torso," I told her and demonstrated. Moving on, I made eye contact with the blonde in pigtails, and said, "The barre is just for balance, and NOT to be leaned upon." She giggled. The raven-haired girl stayed true to my first assessment: her movements were precise, but stilted. She had no animation. "There is more to Classical

Ballet than learning combinations to repeat over and over," I chided with feeling. "The facial expressions, the tilt of your head, and how the hands and arms move is an art. Take care to keep that in mind, girls." I continued to move down the line of dancers, stopping as necessary until I came to Narissa. Her face was red from exertion; sweat ran down her cheeks and neck.

I noticed one of her arms seemed out of proportion and was curved more at the elbow than was necessary, looking more like a circle instead of the oval it needed to be. As I reached down to correct the position, I realized how strangely she was looking at me. It reminded me of how a cat might look the moment before it spooked and ran off. Had I frightened her? I didn't want to be so stern with these girls that they were afraid to ask me a question if they were confused or wanted help.

"I can't," she quickly said before I had even touched her. My heart jerked when she puckered her mouth.

"You can't what?" I decided it best not to touch her as she looked like she might burst into tears. I watched her face struggle for control then for the nerve to talk. She started to say something once, then stopped, waited a moment, then took a breath and started again—only to stop and glance at the other girls. The blonde in the pigtails covered her mouth; it didn't take a college degree to see that she was smiling. The brunette with the fuzzy hair giggled. More girls giggled. Not again, I thought. "Shhh" I warned. "Quiet!"

"I can't straighten my arm," she finally said and held it up for me to see.

I pulled my eyes from the shame I saw etched in her face to study her arm. Yes...I could see now that it had an unnatural curve; the deformity appeared to be a birth defect. How sad, was all I could think. Sophie would definitely be getting a call tonight. Not from any mothers, but from me. This little girl had no business dancing, and if I could, I'd put a stop to it.

"Miss Kayla?" she spoke close to a whisper. "My foot isn't right, either." She lifted her leg and pointed to her ankle. "It's stiff. Dancing helps keep it limber."

Another birth defect? I thought. I stared at her feet. One of her ankles was bigger than the other one. The foot didn't seem right either. She wiggled it, trying to show me its awkwardness. "I see," was all I could think of to say.

"She's crippled," volunteered the redhead. "Didn't you know?"

Again the protective instinct I wasn't even aware I had flared. "She's not crippled!" I snapped unintentionally at the class and paused to take a deep breath, trying to think of another way to describe what I'd seen. "Her body is just formed differently than ours."

Sophie hadn't mentioned Narissa, and I found myself wondering, why?

"My mother says it's too bad," said the blonde in the bun. "She says Nissa shouldn't be taking dance lessons. She says it's a darned shame her mother makes her dance."

I agreed with the blonde in the bun; Narissa really shouldn't be dancing. It obviously humiliated her. But to hear it voiced from children standing right next to Narissa seemed cruel. Children could be so painfully honest. I glanced at my watch and, to my relief, discovered the hour and a half was nearly over. I'd taken more time than I should have showing off. Practicing the Christmas dance would have to wait. I stepped in view of the door and checked the foyer. Another group of students was sitting on the bench getting their ballet slippers on. I touched Narissa on the shoulder. "I want you to stay after," I said to her, and turned and walked back to the middle of the floor.

"Let's get ready to dismiss," I said to the girls, and watched as they formed a straight line in front of me across the floor. "Miss Sophie says you know your Christmas dances. Continue to work on them at home and I will see you back in class on Wednesday. Remember practice makes beautiful dancers." When the class was in position, I took them through the three-step sequence that traditionally ended each class, a dancer's way of saying good-bye, and released them.

The girls in class seemed unaffected by what had happened with Narissa. They left the dance floor laughing and talking, some holding hands. A couple of them even thanked me, though I couldn't remember their names. It would take me longer than the first day of teaching to remember everyone's names.

Narissa walked over to me and waited. The pain and embarrassment I saw in her downcast expression pulled at my insides. She was staring after some of the girls from her class who were now in the foyer talking animatedly and removing their slippers.

"Narissa," I said. She startled when I said her name and looked up at me. "Does your mother make you dance?"

Narissa lowered her head and said nothing, then began wringing her hands as if worried. I bent down, my hands resting on my knees, and tried to get her to look at me. "Does she?" I asked again. Because I knew that if her mother was forcing her to dance and there was no reason for it, she would soon be hearing from me, despite my resolve not to upset Sophie's dance mothers.

Narissa looked at me. "No! It's because I want..." she hesitated, glancing in the direction of the foyer once more. A small group of girls were making their way onto the dance floor. Apparently she didn't want them overhearing.

"What is it you want, Narissa?" I said, lowering my voice.

She leaned forward, near my ear. "I want to dance. I want to be a ballerina."

I looked at the skinny little girl who had been labeled a cripple, and saw something I had missed before. I saw a young girl who had the hope and courage it took to endure the teasing of other dancers, all so that she might have a taste of something she could never have: the gift of dance and grace, the ability to perform a dance to perfection. I felt sorry for her and decided that someone needed to tell her the truth. Perhaps no one had been honest with her? Her mother was probably on a pity party and gave her anything she wanted. Sophie had even indulged Narissa's fantasies, because she had put her in one of the intermediate classes.

Taking hold of Narissa's hand, I squeezed it to show her...what, I wondered? That I cared? Understood how she felt? There were no birth defects on my body. I had never struggled to fit in with other dancers. "Narissa..." I began, and stopped. She was looking at me with those sad eyes, and it was then that I realized she had confided something to me that was very dear to her. I swallowed; it wasn't going to be as easy as I thought to tell her the truth. "What you need to do," I began again, and I paused to clear my throat and think. "I mean..." I couldn't stand it! It wasn't supposed to be this hard to tell the truth. I gave an exasperated sigh. "If you truly want to learn how to dance," I continued, "you must first understand where the gift to dance comes from. It doesn't come from the body at all. It comes from here," and I touched her over her heart, cursing myself silently for my lack of courage. "Someone like you, Narissa, needs to learn to dance from the heart."

The noise in the foyer and on the floor was getting louder. I knew I would have to hurry, but I had remembered something I hadn't thought about in years, and I thought it might be a good idea if I shared it with her. "When I was a little girl, my father took me to see a flock of swans swimming in a narrow river at a park. I loved to see the swans, because to me, the swans were like ballerinas; they were the most elegant creatures in the world and I wanted to be like them. I wanted to possess their grace and beauty. From then on, whenever I got too tired or frustrated and thought that I couldn't do a particular dance step, I'd remember the swans and I'd try harder." I stood and lifted one leg high in the air; arms outstretched, head poised, I held myself in perfect balance. "Until one day, do you know what happened?" I looked down at her. She was staring at me with child-like wonder.

"What?" she said as if hanging on every word.

I gave her a wide smile. "I became the swan!" Stretching my arms out to each side of me, I beat the air slowly, imitating a swan in flight. I knelt down by her then, and took her face in my hands. "I'm going to teach you to dance like a swan, Narissa. But you have to promise me you're going to try harder than you've ever tried in your whole life. Can you do that for me...and for yourself?"

Looking delighted, Narissa nodded eagerly. "Oh yes, Miss Kayla. I'll learn to dance like a swan, even if it hurts!"

I stood and tapped the tip of her nose. "You remember you said that," and I pushed her toward the door.

Four

That night I gave Sophie a call. I told her about my crazy first day, and we had some good laughs. Her laughter made me feel better. But mostly I told her about Narissa's class that day, how the girls had treated her, and what they had said, and discovered Sophie wasn't surprised.

"Why didn't you tell me about her?" I asked.

Sophie hesitated. "It slipped my mind…honestly. But now that you've met her, well, can you see how she has this way of winning you over?"

"Not really," I told Sophie. "I felt sorry for her more than anything else."

"What she really needs is someone to believe in her, to be her friend," she coaxed. "Someone like you."

"I don't want her for a friend! I can't afford to get attached, Sophie."

"Suit yourself."

I decided to change the subject by telling Sophie

what I had told Narissa about the swan. "Do you think I went too far?" I asked her afterwards. "I mean...I lied to her."

"Who knows? Narissa used to dance better than she does now. Lately she's seemed more withdrawn. I hoped that in one of my older classes, she wouldn't be teased as much."

"Why has she seemed more withdrawn? I asked.

Sophie sighed. "Because Narissa's had poor health since birth, and she's always getting sick. I keep expecting her mother to call and tell me she won't be back to class. I know her parents are really concerned about her. Last year Narissa came down with pneumonia. It took her weeks to get better. And she looks paler to me every time I see her, but that's part of her sickness, too, I guess."

Don't get involved, I told myself silently, then asked, "What else is wrong with her?"

"Her mother told me she has an immune disorder," said Sophie.

"Two birth defects and an immune disease, that's a lot for one little girl to overcome."

"Yeah, I know. I really get after my students when I hear any of them call Narissa a cripple. Still, Narissa's going to have to learn to live with cruel remarks. She needs to get tough and be happy with who she is."

She didn't need to tell ME that. I'd witnessed it first hand today. "A skinny cripple who dreams of dancing?" I commented.

"Kayla…"

I could tell from Sophie's voice I'd said the wrong thing. "Maybe it would be better to have Narissa face the truth now, rather than later."

"I see the truth as a little girl who needs a friend and who wants to dance like a swan," she told me.

"Don't forget I'm only a substitute," I reminded her. "But I'll see what I can do."

"Did you decide on any solos yet?" she asked, changing the subject.

I groaned because it had completely slipped my mind. Trying to keep Sophie's dancers under control had been my biggest challenge, and I knew I'd failed miserably even at that.

"No. I'll choose them next week after I've seen more dancing."

"Good. I really appreciate this, Kayla."

She better be grateful, I thought a tad spiteful. After the grueling day I'd been through, I was in need of a hot steaming bath; I had more aches and pains than I did after a company rehearsal. "I'm working it out," I said and tried to sound less whiny and more sincere. I knew my voice lacked enthusiasm, but I was tired. I wasn't looking forward to choosing any dance soloists from her students after today. With more girls than solos, I was bound to have unhappy dancers.

I continued teaching Sophie's students the rest of that week: I broke up two fights, stuffed toilet paper up one eight-year-old's bleeding nose, rosined children's ballet slippers to keep them from slipping on the dance floor, and unclogged the toilet three times, thanking the good Lord each time I went into the bathroom the toilet hadn't run over. To my surprise and my mother's joy, I ate more that week than I had eaten in years.

The weekend was a much-welcomed rest; I think I'd earned it. I actually slept Saturday until noon. My mother had waffles with strawberries and cream fixed for me when I walked downstairs. That may have sounded like a terrible lunch to me a week earlier, but it didn't now. The strawberries smelled fresh and sweet, and the two cinnamon waffles that I ate smothered in maple syrup melted in my mouth. A ring of cream circled my mouth and spotted my nose when I was finished. My mother laughed and told me to go look in the mirror.

"What...what are you talking about?" I said as she pushed me toward the bathroom. When I looked in the mirror at the cream on my face, I rolled my eyes. Was I five? Smiling, I splashed water on my face and returned to my bedroom. Being in my old room after stuffing myself with a home cooked meal brought back nostalgic memories for me—being scolded for not keeping a clean room, early morning chats with Dad before school, late night movies, and the fun trips we used to take as a family. Where had all the time gone, I wondered? Was that little girl still a part of me somewhere? When I was showered and dressed, I pulled a box filled with junk and covered in dust out from under my bed and I sneezed. It had been years since I had looked at any of my treasures; and they were my treasures, I'd just forgotten that I had them.

My mother walked into my room to see what I was doing. She hadn't brought Sophie up—or any of the other grievances she usually hounded me about— since we talked shortly after my arrival home. I didn't say anything to her about it, as I didn't want to light a fuse, but appreciated her ceasefire.

"Sit down," I told her patting my bed. "Let's go through this box for the heck of it." She looked surprised at first, then her face softened and she sat down next to me.

We had fun that afternoon looking at old prom pictures. There wasn't a man in my life and hadn't been for a long while. But seeing myself in a beautiful formal hanging on an old boyfriend's arm sparked emotions that could be thought about later, when my mother and I weren't pointing and smiling, laughing, and pulling weird faces over my memorabilia. We found a red clay heart I had made that had been an old science project. We went through a ballet scrapbook I'd made of the places I wanted to dance when I became a ballerina. I'd glued pictures of myself on famous stages. I found old pointe shoes that smelled of mildew, scuffed and full of holes; a favorite dance costume, black and white with bright red sequins; old hair pieces; and a silver crown. Though the crystals were dim with age, it still sparkled in the light, and I thought of the night I had worn it: Sophie, and another dancer named Autumn, and I had all worn the same crowns and danced like princesses at that particular recital…it was the very night that Sophie and I had pinky promised each other we would never marry, we would be best friends forever and dance until we grew old and died.

When my mother got up off the bed to leave, she leaned over and brushed a kiss across my cheek. We hadn't stopped hugging and kissing as a formality when we saw each other, but this kiss didn't feel hollow, it was filled with the sweet experiences we had shared that afternoon. "I love you, Kayla," she told me.

"Thanks, Mom," I said and squeezed her hand, to let her know I cared, but couldn't bring myself to say it out loud. I loved her too, so why was I being such a hardhead?

Sunday I went to church with my parents. I hadn't done that in years either. My mom and dad were walking out the door when I ran down the stairs to catch up with them. "Wait, I'm coming. I need to grab my coat."

"We'll wait," Dad said, and I saw him reach for my mother's hand.

We took a drive after dinner to my favorite park, the place where I had first seen the swans in the river. The air was crisp and chill, and I was saddened because I knew there would be no swans there now. As we were walking near the narrow river, I thought of Narissa. She would be a challenge, and that scared me...

When Monday afternoon came around again, as unexpected as this new feeling was, I found myself looking forward to Sophie's dance classes, except for Narissa. I had mixed feelings about seeing her. Still, I had thought up some special exercises I intended to give her during class.

I arrived at the studio earlier than the week before. After warming up at the dance barre, stretching my legs and arms, and dancing a short piece from a performance, I went over my notes. Combined with Sophie's instructions, I had a good workable idea of what I wanted to accomplish that day.

As the dancers for my first class stepped through the front door into the foyer and removed their coats, boots, hats, and other clothing articles, I greeted them, asked them to put on their ballet shoes, and promptly sent them onto the dance floor to warm up. I hoped that by doing this, I'd cut down on the noise and confusion of last week. Most of them minded me; a few didn't listen and began talking, which considering their young ages was probably normal. So I repeated myself, trying to portray a confidence in myself that wasn't present last week. I wrapped my arm around Alicia, and in a low whisper told her to visit the bathroom before class. When Darren farted in the foyer and laughed, looking around to see what young beauty had noticed and was reacting with the repulsion he hoped to see, I reminded him in front of those watching that handsome male dancers like him didn't do those kinds of things, that he was better off using any extra wind he possessed for doing great leaps. He certainly didn't want any of the girls out-jumping him. I hated to admit it, but I had a new respect for Sophie's teaching abilities; it wasn't every dancer who could teach children to dance.

When it came time to teach Narissa's class, she was one of the last girls to arrive. She kept her head down when she came shuffling out onto the floor to take her place at the barre. No one spoke to her.

When it was time, I pounded my stick and class began. After a good warm-up to stretch the muscles, work the tendons, and loosen the joints by doing a series of pliés, leg stretches, and footwork, I had them move away from the barre for center practice. I hoped that my new exercises would develop a better sense of balance and fluidity of movement. We lay with our backs on the floor and pushed our feet against the wall, first the heels and then the toes. We walked up the wall imitating Spiderman ten times. We stood up and jumped on one leg, then the other, trying to catch the tail of a kite. We became human rubber and bounced like balls on our feet, pushing higher and higher, until we touched the clouds. We picked apples in a tree and stretched our arms to reach those on the highest branches. Narissa, like the rest, seemed willing to try something new. I walked down the line of dancers correcting arms and feet as needed. When I stepped up to Narrisa and reached to correct her arm, she didn't try to avoid me. I touched her, ran my fingers down the imperfection of her arm, and smoothed out the tightness I felt there as best as I could by rubbing her muscles. Sweat rolled down her brow and she gave me a puppy dog face.

I winked because I couldn't help myself. "Well done," I told her using my best teacher's voice for the benefit of the other dancers watching us.

When we started rehearsing for the Christmas recital, I had her push forward with her shoulder, compensating for the unnatural curve of her arm. It seemed to work; Narissa looked less awkward, more centered. We both smiled over that one. "See!" I said, and she nodded.

Toward the end of class, as I watched the girls practice their Christmas dance, I realized Sophie had been right about her classes; her students knew their recital dances, including the solos, but needed more practice...lots more practice. I loved Sophie's choice of Christmas songs for her dancers: *Rudolf the Red Nosed Reindeer*, *Here Comes Santa Claus*, *White Christmas*, *Away in a Manger*, *Oh Come All Ye Faithful*, and *The First Noel* were my favorites...until I listened to *Silent Night*. The song was perfect for this class, the music slow and dream-filled, easier for Narissa to dance to.

Right at the moment, however, some of them were having problems keeping up with the music. I slowed it down, and we started over. Narissa's jetés looked much better. At least, when she leapt from one foot onto the other she didn't look like a spinning top ready to tip over. I told them that to keep their balance, they needed to remember to dance on all five of their toes, to think about each toe and where it was as they moved.

The other girls danced better, too; their movements appeared more fluid and their bodies better balanced. I could see why Sophie thought Jenny, the blonde with the bun, might be the right dancer for the solo in this class. Her natural ability soared over the rest; her extensions were higher, straighter, and her movements much less jerky. She kept her balance like a true intermediate dancer.

The girls performed two pirouettes in the middle

of their dance. As they turned a third to complete the sequence before the solo began, Narissa stumbled. Thinking she would fall, even get hurt, I rushed forward to catch her and knocked Jenny onto her bottom. Swearing under my breath, watching as Narissa regained her balance, I turned to help Jenny.

"Jenny! I'm so sorry." I bent down and pulled her to her feet.

Fists clenched and red faced, Jenny stood and glared at Narissa. "You clumsy oaf!" she screamed. "I'm sick of you!"

"Jenny!" I said. "Please don't talk like that!"

Jenny turned to me and blew the bangs from her face. She couldn't have been noisier if she had tried. "Nobody wants to dance around her. She trips people!"

"I pushed you down, Jenny, not Narissa." Face red with embarrassment or exhaustion, Jenny's cruel remarks now had Narissa staring quietly at the floor, her hands clasped tightly in front of her, as if she were a convicted felon awaiting her sentence.

"But it was her fault!" screamed Jenny, pointing at Narissa and stomping her feet. "She shouldn't be dancing!"

I'd heard enough. No one, not even a young, perfect-looking girl, had the right to tear down another human being like that. I was furious. "It's too bad you feel that way, Jenny." I looked from her to the rest of the class. "I was going to wait until class was over, but I might as well tell you all now. The first solo in the Christmas recital this year goes to Narissa Serveen. I hope you'll all support her." Appearing confused, Narissa glanced at me before slowly dropping her head again.

"You can't!" Hands on her hips, Jenny puffed up like a fish I'd seen once in an aquarium. "You can't give the solo to a cripple! Miss Sophie says—"

"That's enough!" I interrupted, glaring back. "No more!"

And it was enough, because Jenny whirled around and stormed out of the room, mumbling things about telling her mother and father...that I'd be fired...that Narissa would be kicked out of their class...things that I tried not to let bother me, but they did. Striking the floor with my stick for attention, I promptly dismissed the class even though it was ten minutes early. "Practice your Christmas dance," I told them as the dancers walked off the floor, knowing they would run straight to their parents with the latest news. As I watched the girls leave, I wished somehow that I could turn back the clock. My mother used to tell me when I was younger that one day my temper would get the best of me...maybe she was right. What had I just done?

Narissa waited until the room was empty before

walking up to me. She had to pull on my hand to get my attention. "You didn't have to do that." She looked apologetic and worried enough for us both. "I know I'm not good enough." She paused for a moment, and in a voice so soft that I could barely hear she said, "You can give the solo to Jenny. I won't get mad."

Sweet relief washed over me, and I dropped to my knees and stared at her. I hadn't wanted to make a mistake, and yet, I was afraid that with Narissa, I had.

"You don't want to dance the solo?" I asked.

Narissa started to shake her head then stopped. She studied me, staring intently into my eyes. Something clicked inside of her, a softening in her face, because I knew without doubt that Narissa had decided to trust me with what she was about to say, and I couldn't help feeling that it was very important. "I DO want to dance the solo. I want to be a swan, like you. But..." She glanced at her foot, at her arm, then back at me and sniffled. "I can never be a swan, not really."

The defeat I heard in her voice tore at my very soul. I couldn't stand it. I had to do something. I wanted to cry. "But you *can* be a swan!" I argued. "You can be good enough! We proved that today. Didn't we?" She nodded, and I did something that surprised even me: I hugged her. A strand of hair had fallen from her ponytail, and I pulled it from her face, suppressing the sudden need I had to kiss her cheek. "Work hard every day, Narissa. Your next class we'll work some more. Keep doing the exercises I showed you. You'll get it! You'll see!" Smiling, I turned her toward the door and pushed her along. "Now scoot, little swan. I've got another class to teach."

Narissa walked as far as the foyer before turning back around. She saw me watching her. Still, neither of us said a word. She stared at me momentarily, gave me a small smile, and then raised her arms, stretching them high as if picking an apple. She whirled and giggled, then waved 'bye. I waved back, stood up, and began pounding my stick.

Five

*T*he telephone was ringing as I stepped into my parents' home that evening. My dancer's intuition told me it would be Sophie, and I was right. Before I could say anything, Sophie told me she had heard all about it from a mother.

"Jenny's?" I asked.

Sophie chuckled. She didn't seem as upset as I thought she might be.

"So what happened?"

Sophie grunted. "Jenny's mother threatened to pull Jenny out of class if I didn't set things straight with you about Narissa."

"And what did you say?"

"I told her that Narissa was who I had chosen for the solo, and that I was sorry if it was going to cause her any inconvenience."

I whooped so loud I almost dropped the phone. "Thanks for backing me up."

"You've made a terrible mistake," my mother said from behind me when I was finished talking with Sophie and I'd hung up the phone. She had a dishtowel draped over her right shoulder and what looked like a spray of flour on her clothes and hands. She'd obviously stepped out of the kitchen and overheard the conversation.

So my mother wasn't on my side. Couldn't I do anything right? "What do you mean?" I asked her.

"If Jenny is really the best dancer in that class, then Jenny deserves the lead. Don't set yourself or Narissa up for a disappointment, Kayla. You can count on a dancer like Jenny. Narissa lacks the experience. She'll be just as happy with a simpler part."

When it came to dance my mother was dependably pragmatic. "Stay out of it, Mom."

"You wouldn't say that to your father. Why say it to me?"

My dad was out of town on business for a week — some big insurance conference in Las Vegas for top agents. When he'd come to kiss me good-bye, I told him that it was dangerous to leave Mom and I alone together in the same house without him. And I was right! Arguing with my mother tore me apart inside. "Because Daddy believes in me!"

"How can you say that? I believe in you!"

I held my hands out in front of me, as if staving off an attack. "*Please,* leave it alone!"

"You always talk to your father. Talk to ME, Kayla."

I didn't want to get into this right now; our relationship was doing better. "Why don't you go cook something," I said waving her away. Cooking gave my mother other things to think about. She didn't seem as bossy when she cooked. I immediately regretted the comment though, after seeing her wounded expression. "You really want to know why I talk to Dad more?"

She placed her hands on her hips and braced herself like she was a captain on a ship expecting strong winds. "Yeah! I really want to know."

Maybe my mother finally did want to hear the truth. Maybe dealing with Narissa was giving me courage now...the strength to open up and actually talk honestly with her. Frustration rose like lava spewing from a volcano. I needed to either run up the stairs to my room and slam the door or face her. "You never listen to me! It doesn't matter what I say, you—"

"I listen to you!" interrupted my mother.

Tamping down my emotions, I took a deep breath. "No, Mom, you don't. You didn't just now." Tears came unbidden to my eyes. "You could never just be my friend and listen...tell me my ideas were okay sometimes, laugh once in a while when I made a mistake, cry when I hurt and tell me that one way or another things would work out for the best." I laughed at her, but it was more of an unhappy rumble. I didn't want to cry, but what did that matter? "You're incredible, Mom. You've got a lot of strength and determination. You're really smart. I admire you more than you'll ever know. But I'm strong and smart too, or at least, I've always tried to be. Why can't you ever make me feel like it's okay to be me?"

"And Daddy does?"

I didn't want to hurt her. But I'd come too far to turn back now. "Yes. Daddy does. He listens with his heart."

"I love you!" she said like a person drowning.

For the first time in years, I wanted to reach out and hug her, to feel her tenderness, but the fear of her rejection kept me from moving. Old habits die hard. "I love you, too!" I managed to say. Yet, it was too late. I saw the pain behind her eyes and knew that she had misread my fear, that she saw it as her own failure.

"Mom..."

She sighed and backed away, hands patting vacant air. "I need to think." She walked back into the kitchen before I could say another word.

I didn't follow her. A little space might do us both some good. Besides, it wouldn't hurt to do a little thinking of my own.

As I continued to teach Sophie's classes and have her students work on their individual dances for the Christmas recital, the week flew by. On Wednesday Narissa didn't act like herself in class; she danced much slower and kept wheezing. I asked her if she was feeling okay, and she assured me that she was fine. Allergies? I wondered. Narissa was probably so thrilled about her solo that even if she'd been sick, she had determined not to quit that day. The little girl with the black bun had a cold and kept sneezing on everyone in class. I hoped we didn't get sick.

Saturday afternoon I took a long walk dressed in a borrowed pair of Mom's winter boots, a snug-fitting wool hat, and warm gloves that had rabbit fur around the edges. Winter had definitely settled down in the valley for a long cozy nap. Foot-high snow covered dead lawns and hung like white shorn wool in trees.

As I stepped through the snow, a calming peace overwhelmed me, seeped in through hidden cracks, and my eyes filled with unshed tears. Christmas was just around the corner.

Six

*L*ater that evening I called Sophie, but she and David weren't home. I hoped she was okay. If she was on bed rest, why wasn't she near a phone? My mother was out Christmas shopping. I was grateful that I'd already done mine. I hated the crowds and mass confusion that came with holiday shopping. After folding and putting away a load of my laundry, doing a sink filled with dishes, and fixing myself a yummy cucumber sandwich, I went into the family room and snuggled down in Dad's favorite leather recliner to read. I had just pulled a random book off of the shelf, and only now glanced at the title, *Sink Reflections: The Fly Lady's Simple Flying Lessons will Show You How to Get Your Home in Order — and it All starts with Shining Your Sink!* I smiled in amusement after reading the front cover; it starts with the sink, huh? I tried reading for several minutes then gave up. Pictures of shining sinks were boring no matter how clean they were.

Most of Sunday afternoon was spent with my nose buried in a delicious fantasy novel I'd rescued off of the family room bookshelf, after being suffocated by a group of self-help books, poor thing. I made a note to check with Barnes and Noble the following afternoon to see what other books had been written by that particular author. Top on my list, after the Christmas recital, would be to spoil myself and buy more fantasy books to sink my teeth into. Not before. I needed to focus all of my time, energy, and attention on getting Sophie's dancers through their performances, and helping Narissa survive her solo.

That evening my mother and I sat watching television in the family room when my father walked through the front door. Mom and I were speaking to each other, just no 'heart to heart' conversation that might cause friction. She had popped some popcorn, heavy on the butter, and we were sharing it.

"Ho! Ho! Ho!" he called out playfully. "I'm home and bring good tidings of great joy." Stomping the wet snow from his feet, he walked through the hallway dragging a scrawny odd-shaped Christmas tree—branches missing in places that left gaping holes—like he'd just brought us each a rare piece of jade from China.

I got up from the couch and went to greet him. "Hey, Dad," I said giving him an awkward one-armed hug since he was holding the tree.

"You aren't going to believe this," my dad said dropping the pine tree on the floor and brushing his hands off on his pants, "but on my way home from the airport tonight, about a mile from the house..." he gestured over his shoulder, and glanced at my mother and me, as if completely baffled, "there leaning against a fence was this tree. On the ground by the tree was a big piece of white cardboard with writing on it that said *FREE!* I pulled off to the side of the road to check things out. It was dark enough that I had to put on my glasses and read it twice to make sure I'd read it correctly. Crazy, huh?"

I looked over at my mother, who stood staring open mouthed at the ugly tree and the snow that would soon melt into puddles on her clean floor. My mother was an elegant woman who enjoyed pretty things. She and my dad usually chose the tree together in December, but never BEFORE Thanksgiving. When I was living at home, the three of us always went as a family to get our tree, which was usually the most beautiful tree on the lot, not necessarily the most expensive, but definitely one filled with branches and tall enough that my dad would need a ladder to set the Christmas star on the top. My mother could hang the star this year if she wanted, as no ladder would be needed.

"Well," he said to us, "what do you think?" He acted like an excited little boy waiting to open presents on Christmas morning.

This had to be the funkiest tree we'd ever had. Dad and I turned in unison to look at my mother, who swiveled her head from left to right imitating a robin in a tree and said after quiet deliberation, "Bob...I think this tree is perfect." Her face softened and she looked at my dad with tenderness.

My dad clapped his hands. "I'll get the tree stand

and get it set up. You guys start pulling the Christmas boxes out from under the basement stairs."

On Monday, the week of Thanksgiving, I posted a handwritten sign on the studio door that announced to the dancers there would be no classes held after Wednesday, and they wouldn't resume again until the following Monday. I even sent reminders home with each dancer, worried that parents wouldn't read my sign.

Thanksgiving was like so many I'd had in the past. Grandma and Grandpa Davis came over for dinner. Grandma brought pumpkin and blackberry pies with fresh whipped cream. Mom made her famous baked beans and shrimp cocktail salad. When the turkey was ready to eat, Grandpa said the blessing. And we all ate until we couldn't eat any more. I fell asleep on the couch and blamed it on the turkey; all those hormones they feed those dang birds. Certainly was worth it, though.

Friday and Saturday were crazy days. People suddenly forgot about Thanksgiving and began planning for Christmas. Mom's turkey and pilgrim decorations came down and were quickly replaced by ones that depicted the Christmas season. I stepped outside once to take out the garbage, and noticed the rest of our neighbors were carbon copies of my mother. Several men, young and old, busied themselves outside their homes wrapping Christmas lights in their trees, hanging lights along fences, across doorways and framing beautiful windows with richly decorated Christmas trees peeking outside. Wreaths hung on doors…artificial holly, red and green bows, tiny dolls and Santa Clauses, golden harps, glass angels…I loved it all. Christmas is such a special time of the year, I thought. There's not another holiday like it. I'd almost forgotten. A teenager drove by me with Christmas lights actually blinking in his rear window. A group of children played in their yard rolling snow and building a snowman, their black Labrador barking and nipping at their feet. A little boy with bright red cheeks wearing a blue parka waved at me and I waved back.

By the following week I was pretty settled into a sort of routine. During the days, I split up my time between helping my mother with a charity sewing project, which was making baby blankets and quilts for a homeless shelter; helping her wrap Christmas presents for friends and family members; shopping with her for neighborhood gifts to pass out; going with her to visit my grandparents who lived in

Ockerville, a small town north of Stansbury; helping her plan and organize their church Christmas party (since Mom was the head of the committee); going to lunch with a few old high school friends I hadn't seen in years; and shoveling my parents' driveway and sidewalks a time or two.

My afternoons and evenings, however, were solely devoted to teaching at Sophie's dance studio. After nearly three weeks of teaching, I found that I quite enjoyed the challenges that came with the job. I made a practice of getting to the studio early each day to warm up and prepare mentally. Like a well-trained drill sergeant, I ran a tight camp. I started out each class with warm-ups, moved on to barre exercises, then center floor practice, and finally worked on recital numbers. The rest of the soloists had been chosen and were working on their parts in class. At times I felt like a seasoned referee, calling out fouls, breaking up fights, drying tears and soothing hurt feelings. I constantly reminded certain students to work at being nicer to one another.

During Narissa's practices, I made sure she did more exercises, trying not to give her special treatment or attention, but working with her individually only when I could see she was having a harder time keeping up with the other girls.

Everyone participated except Jenny, who was absent for both classes that week. I marveled a couple different times at Narissa's iron will; her hair matted down with sweat and out of breath by the end of each class, yet she practiced so very hard in class and on her Christmas solo. The steps weren't difficult for someone without Narissa's issues, but definitely more challenging for her. Still, she allowed me to tuck a leg, reposition her body when she needed it, and adjust her arms. I actually caught the redhead correcting Narissa's foot, the blonde in pigtails offering words of encouragement and approval. "That's the way, Nissa. You've *got* it now."

Narissa smiled happily at us all.

Wednesday's practice I had Narissa sit down on the floor so I could rub her ankle and foot afterwards. Her spirits seemed higher, and for that I was grateful. "There...done," I said as I patted her legs. "You looked beautiful today. I'm very pleased."

"Like a swan?" she said softly, quietly waiting for my answer.

"Almost," I told her and touched her lightly on the nose. "I see some feathers...here," I touched each cheek, "and here and here." I touched her on her back, smiling. "Yes," I said, looking her over carefully, "there's a swan in there...I see her emerging..."

She stood and hugged me.

I hugged her back.

Mom picked me up after my classes. She seemed to understand that after listening to children all afternoon it felt good to ride home in silence. Dinner was quiet too, for a change. It was nice listening to my parents talk without feeling like I needed to take part in their conversation to make my mother happy. I suspected my father had something to do with it. Donning my winter coat later that evening I walked outside, shut the door, and immediately smelled burning wood that made me think of cozy fires and hot cider...and one incredible year when my father had been laid off of work and the three of us had made brightly colored popcorn balls to hang on our tree that we ate throughout the holidays...until they grew too hard to eat—but by that time there weren't many left.

The night was alive with Christmas spirit. Across the street a group of carolers, maybe fifteen of them, young men and women dressed in warm clothes, carrying antique cow bells that tinkled loudly as they walked, knocked on the Jorgensen's door. I could hear their playful banter and the shushing of someone in their crowd, getting them organized and quieted enough to sing. I couldn't help myself. I stopped walking to listen. A door opened and voices gentle and soft, no longer teasing, rose in unison and began singing a Christmas song that I had loved singing as a girl—Silent night...Holy night...all is calm...all is bright...uncanny, I thought, that Narissa would be dancing a solo to this same song. I walked down the street humming the tune under my breath.

Brushing the snow from my feet I walked into the front door an hour later. My hands were freezing, and my toes and face were numb. My nose ran like a faucet, but I felt refreshed, calmer.

Seven

*T*hursday afternoon disaster struck. A five-year-old student, Amber, brought a pet hamster in her dance bag to show her friend. It got loose during class and ran across the floor. Screams filled the air simultaneously as boys and girls chased the troublesome varmint, which by some quirk of nature managed to avoid all of their jumping feet. We spent the last half of class looking for it, but it wasn't found. She whispered in my ear before leaving that her hamster's name was Buttercup, and she was going to have babies. I decided to leave that one for Sophie to solve.

Friday after lunch Sophie called to tell me she was in labor; the baby was coming early. I experienced excitement over her pregnancy for the first time. I called Jan Stevens and had her cancel dance classes immediately.

I spent the afternoon pacing the hospital floor outside the birthing rooms, trying not to think of that stupid dream I'd had. I had time to say hello to Sophie when I got there, tell her that her students were doing great, and kiss her on the forehead before a nurse asked me if I was staying for the birth. Sophie didn't invite me, and I wasn't entirely certain that she needed me there, so I shook my head.

"There's a waiting room around the corner," she told me in a kind but bossy tone. "It's close to this room."

I may not have been invited to stay in the room with Sophie, but I wasn't going around that corner out of earshot. I grabbed a chair that sat in the hallway and parked myself outside of her door. Nurses went in and out of her room for hours. The waiting area did have some magazines, though. I helped myself and went back to my chair before someone moved it.

I heard Sophie moaning and David's mumbles through the door several times, hoping that if her discomfort wasn't part of the birthing process, someone would let me know. A handsome, broad shouldered guy, with a black beard and deep blue eyes, walked down the hall around nine o'clock that evening and into her room carrying a clipboard. Even in green scrubs he was the spitting image of the guy I'd envisioned in the romance novel I'd read in my parent's library. Was that Sophie's doctor? Not fair! Growing up, for check-ups, physicals or when I'd been really sick, I had seen a family doctor who wore bug glasses that made his eyeballs look too big, a pot belly that reminded me of Santa Claus, and had a partially bald head with short, spiky white hair. I wondered if my parents still used that doctor, or if he was retired? Thinking of Dr. Delicious, I decided that if they didn't need a new doctor I just might...but what was I thinking? After the holidays I was flying right back to New York City and getting on with the life I'd made for myself.

"Is she okay?" I finally asked one of the nurses going into her room.

"Sure," said the nurse. "The nurse anesthetist is giving her an epidural right now. She's dilating fast now, but Dr. Matheson will be here any moment, and then we'll have a baby."

"You mean the guy that went in there isn't her baby doctor?" I asked her, pointing a finger at the door.

Older and a bit overweight—just like in my dream—she raised her eyebrow, peering at me like a woman who knew what I was really asking...*is he single and available?* Then she shook her head. "No. He's our new anesthetist." She put a hand to her mouth and leaned toward me conspiratorially. "He's not married."

When the anesthetist left, he glanced at me and winked. Winked? I blushed and caught myself staring after him as he sauntered off. I lifted my hand and dramatically slapped the side of my head. What's wrong with me? *I am not a fifteen-year-old girl with a first crush.* Then again, he did have amazing eyes. With a silly grin on my face I sat back down, tucking the image of Mr. Delicious winking at me, in the dashing scrubs, safely inside me for a later date.

The doctor finally arrived. He took quick long strides into the room and shut the door. Sophie was ready and eager to push, if the sounds that were coming from the birthing room were anything to go by. I listened to her talking to David, grunting, calling out; to the doctor talking to her; the nurses counting… Push!…more grunting…more pushing…it sounded like a madhouse inside that birthing room. The noise sounded awful. What was she having…a cow or a baby? Sophie's parents arrived just as a baby's cry pierced the birthing confusion and began exercising its lungs.

Sophie gave birth to a baby boy early Saturday morning three minutes after midnight. Feeling like I'd been run over by a Mac truck, anxious to congratulate Sophie and David so that I could go home and get to bed, the thought of telling Sophie's students about the baby excited me, especially Narissa. She would be delighted.

The nurse on duty allowed Sophie's parents and I to enter the room per Sophie's request shortly after she'd given birth. I followed behind her parents, and once inside went to stand beside a recliner to the left of Sophie and away from all the electronic machines. Sophie looked over at me and smiled. Her face was red and puffy, eyes swollen like she'd been crying, and I couldn't help thinking she had never looked more beautiful. She glanced over to where the baby now lay under a warming light in a clear plastic basinet. Two nurses were putting ointment in his eyes, stretching out his tiny little form to take measurements, and giving him a quick sponge bath; they put a little undershirt on that covered his hands, talking softly to him, and then wrapped him like a burrito in a blue blanket.

As I stood watching, spellbound by the small bundled miracle that had just come into the world, Sophie reached out her hands. The nurse smiled at her impatience, and laid the baby into her waiting arms. "Hi there, little guy. It's Mommy," she cooed and rubbed her nose against his tiny cheek.

Enchanted, she snuggled the calm infant lying peacefully next to her body. "Come see him, Kayla," she said, gently taking hold of one of his fingers. "He's so sweet...he's going to be a dairy farmer...just like his daddy."

Heaven help us, I thought. Why couldn't he be a dancer like his mother? Leaning over her I studied her new son. His big beautiful eyes were wide open and looked back at me cross-eyed as he puckered his mouth. "He's a handsome little guy," I told her.

The doctor and nurses were still there and reminded me of worker ants in an ant colony as they busied themselves with tasks I'm certain were all in a day's work for them.

"Why don't you let Daddy hold him for a minute while we get you cleaned up," the heavyset nurse said. She picked up the baby and handed him to David. He looked stunned momentarily, and then smiled down at his son. He turned to Sophie, lowering the baby so she could see him too. "You did good, babe."

The baby started fussing, trying to suck on his tiny fist. David chuckled tenderly. "I'd forgotten how small they are."

Another nurse stepped up and began massaging Sophie's stomach like she was kneading bread dough. I stepped back to the recliner to give Sophie some privacy and asked the nurse why she was doing that. She explained that it helped retract the uterus. "I'm going to ask you all to step out into the hall for just a minute while we get Sophie cleaned up and change her bedding," she said to everyone in the room.

Sophie's parents each gave her a hug and left.

"Love you," she told them.

The stocky nurse took the baby from David and returned him to the clear basinet.

David walked over to Sophie and kissed her. "I'm going to get something to eat. See you soon."

"Love you," Sophie told him as he walked to the door.

I stepped over to Sophie's bed and squeezed her hand. Sophie pulled me closer and threw her arms around my neck. "Thank you, Kayla." Her eyes filled with tender water, the kind that melts your heart and makes you form water of your own.

My throat tightened and I wondered why I was so emotional when it was Sophie who had given birth? It was time to leave before I turned into a blubbering idiot. "I'm going to head home so that you can get some rest and spend some time with David and the baby," I told her.

"Do you have to go?" she asked.

I smiled because she looked half asleep and utterly exhausted. "I'll be back tomorrow if they haven't sent you and the baby home by then. Would you like me to bring you anything? Something good to eat?"

She shook her head. "No. I've got everything I need. David's a big treat guy; he'll keep me well fed."

"Get some rest then," I ordered her and left.

I was so tired when I got back to my parents' house, I trudged up the stairs and went straight to bed. Sleep evaded me though, and I woke feeling sluggish. I couldn't quit thinking about everything that had happened in my life since I'd gotten home for the holidays. Being a substitute dance teacher and having a best friend give birth was tough work. My parents were delighted to hear over breakfast that Sophie's baby had arrived safely and was in robust health.

I drove to the hospital Saturday afternoon during visiting hours, parked the car, and after making a quick stop at the hospital gift shop went up to Sophie's room. I knocked on the door before entering and could hear a small child giggling and then shortly after, a crash. A grin slid across my face. It sounded like Sophie's parents had brought Ellie, David and Sophie's bouncy four-year-old daughter for a visit too.

"Who's there?" Sophie called cheerfully.

I opened the door and peeked around the corner, holding a stuffed teddy bear behind my back. "Hello?" Sophie's mother sat in a chair next to the bed.

"Kayla, it's good to see you! Come in," Anne exclaimed standing up and walking over to me. "Things were so crazy last night that I didn't get to give you a proper hug." She threw her arms around me and squeezed. "It has been way too long, young lady."

I wanted to roll my eyes but didn't. When I was a girl, Anne always fussed over me, and I didn't like it then or now. "It's good to see you, Mrs. Hepworth." I turned to smile at John as he pulled Ellie down from a chair she had scooted over to the sink. "You too, Mr. Hepworth."

Ellie turned and gave us all a frown.

"Hello, Ellie, are you excited to have a baby brother?" I asked. Appearing shy, she glanced from me to David, who sat in the recliner holding their new son, and reached out for her grandfather's leg, hiding her face against him peek-a-boo style.

"She doesn't know what to think about her new brother," said Sophie and our gazes met.

"I hope I'm not intruding."

"Heavens no!" said Anne. "You're like a second daughter to me."

Sophie nodded in agreement. "Never. Would you like to hold Tyler?"

"Ah..." I hesitated briefly then replied, "sure," in a voice that told everyone in the room newborn's were not my specialty, and any tiny human made me a tad nervous.

David stood carefully so I could take his place in the recliner. When he handed Tyler to me, I quickly dropped the gift I'd brought in the recliner and held out both arms. My hands were shaking. I tried to be very careful, as his blanket wrapped body felt so fragile. Perching on the edge of the recliner, as near to Sophie as I could get, I marveled at their baby. "He's so tiny!" I exclaimed. "Look at all that black hair!"

"He didn't get that from our side of the family," said John. "Our kids were all born bald."

Tyler yawned then scrunched up his face and began rooting around in the blanket. "He's so adorable," I told them and watched as Ellie crawled up on the bed to sit on top of Sophie. "You're adorable too, Ellie." I gave her a soft smile.

She looked from me to her brother. "My baby!" she told me.

We all laughed and I knew the happiness I felt for Sophie and her family was genuine. My anger was gone. Teaching children to dance, laughing and playing with them, working with them, and sharing in many of their frustrations had replaced much of the bitterness and given me a quiet sense of satisfaction; it was like eating an ice cream cone that tasted exactly the way you thought it should.

Tyler let out a loud squeaky cry and began squirming, struggling to free his arms and legs from his blanket. He obviously wanted something from me I couldn't give. "I better go. I've still got errands to run," I said to them and stood.

David held his arms out and took Tyler from me.

I walked over to Sophie and hugged her, handing her the plush teddy bear for little Tyler. Ellie grabbed hold of her mother's hospital gown and yelled at me. "My momma!"

"Yes, your momma," I told her, trying my best to sound agreeable.

"Thanks, Kayla, for stopping by and for the cute gift," said Sophie, setting the bear next to a bundle of white roses and a bag of Snickers Bars I assumed David had given her.

"You're welcome, Soph. See you soon." I waved good-bye to everyone as I turned and walked out the door.

Eight

Mom and Dad drove to the hospital for a look themselves early that evening. "You should have seen your father coddling and talking baby talk to little Tyler. He would make the cutest grandpa," she told me when they had returned. Mom looked at me with hopeful eyes, and then opened the front closet and hung up her coat. She bustled into the kitchen and started setting the table.

I grimaced over her not-so-subtle hint. "I am certain Dad will make an awesome grandpa," I said loud enough that she could hear me...and pictured strapping young boys with jet black hair—minus a beard, green scrubs, and piercing blue eyes.

Mom walked out of the kitchen, wrapped her arms around me, and sighed. "Tyler reminds me of when you were a baby," she said. "Lots of dark hair sticking straight up off your head, only you were much prettier."

Oddly enough my mother and I hadn't argued during the week. She had fixed some delicious meals for me, and we'd held a checker tournament with my dad. Sophie's newborn was alive and well. And even if I still had a great deal of work to do, Sophie's

Christmas recital was coming along nicely. Life felt right. I finished helping her set the table.

Mom had prepared a crock pot stew with hot biscuits and homemade cherry jam (her own secret recipe) for dinner. We sat down at the table and stuffed ourselves. Later, I challenged my dad to a game of checkers. He beat me twice. My mother got up from the couch where she had been reading and walked into the kitchen. She returned moments later carrying a tray laden with three bowls heaped with homemade apple cobbler and vanilla ice cream.

"I'm going to be fatter than I pig when I leave here," I told her. As we ate, I told my parents about Narissa and several of the other children I'd gotten to know. We had a good laugh over Darren, who was now leaping higher than any girl in class without passing gas, and poor Amber's lost hamster. Before parting for the evening, I felt compelled to tell them about my progress with Narissa and the exercises I'd come up with to help her. I was so proud of the way the other dancers were working with her; they seemed happier, more together. Narissa no longer stared at the floor during class. The smile that lit her face when she danced with the others was infectious; everyone seemed to smile more.

"She melts your heart," said my mother studying me.

"A big pool of butter," added my dad.

At one time if my mother had said something like that to me, I might have gotten offended, asked her if she thought I had a heart that needed melting. We might have had a heated discussion with one of us walking away to avoid more frustration and anger. But my mother was right. Narissa did melt my heart. As I recalled the last dance class, the one before Sophie had given birth to Tyler, I saw her straining to practice the Christmas dance with the other girls. "Her self-confidence has grown," I explained to my parents, "yet she still hesitates when dancing her solo in class, then stares at the others as if to reassure herself that what she's doing is correct."

"Doesn't watching the other girls help?" my mother asked.

"Not really. It keeps her one to two beats behind everyone else, and makes it doubly hard for the others to get their timing correct. It amazed me that after class the other day not one dancer complained."

"So what are you going to do?" asked my mother when I finished talking.

I knew what she was doing because it wasn't like her to ask my opinion without first telling me what she thought was best, then insisting her way was the only way: she was asking me to give her a chance; it was a beginning.

I shrugged and gave her an honest answer. "I have no idea."

"You'll figure it out," she said and began gathering the ice cream dishes.

No comments about Narissa's solo and it being a terrible mistake. No I-told-you-so glare. No arguing back and forth. No anger, nothing.

"Thanks, Mom," I said.

"You're welcome." She hesitated, like she wanted to say more but had decided against it.

My father's mouth was still slightly ajar when she turned and walked into the kitchen. I gave him a cat-that-ate-the-canary smile and followed her. While she emptied the dishwasher, I started sweeping the floor. Trust seemed to be filling the empty spaces old fears were leaving behind. My mother was finally listening to me, and that meant more than any amount of money my parents had ever spent helping me pursue a career.

Restless, I slipped on my coat and boots, pulled my hat over my head, and stepped outside for a walk. The snow was light and fluffy and crunched under my boots. I lifted my face skyward, allowing its icy freshness to fall on my cheeks and eyelashes; it felt wonderful. As I ambled down the sidewalks, I admired the many different Christmas trees in the front windows of the houses; each tree reflected the uniqueness of the family that had decorated it. Blinking lights, colorful ornaments that shimmered, angels that bugled at the top of trees; Christmas is nearly here, I thought. After the recital I will no longer be teaching Sophie's students. Surprisingly, this made me sad.

I began to pass by one house but stopped because the tree displayed in this window was different than anything I had seen tonight. It had the limbs carved out of its middle. Straw had been tucked inside the cavity, creating a hollowed out space to make room for a manger scene. The three wise men sitting on their camels and the gifts they bore to the Christ child had been wired to the branches and hung as if suspended within the manger and straw. A bright star shone down from the top of the tree that was lit so beautifully through the figurines it stole my breath for an instant. Animal ornaments—donkeys, sheep, camels, cows, doves—dangling from metal hooks were the only other decorations. I left when a little girl looked out the window at me; hands against the cold glass and open mouthed, she ran away as if to tattle on the peeping stranger.

Nine

Catching a cold was just plain unlucky, especially since I didn't have time for one. I climbed out of bed Monday morning with my chest feeling tight, voice a little hoarse, and feeling tired and achy. My mother was out for the morning with some friends, so I returned to bed until it was time to get dressed and go to the studio. That afternoon while teaching, I felt dizzy and disoriented, and the pressure building in my sinuses and ears made the children's talking sound funny. Instead of heading back to my parents' house after dance classes that evening, I decided that if I wanted to nip this cold before it started I needed to get to a drugstore fast. I locked the studio door and began to walk to the S.O.S. Drugstore instead of driving, as it was only a couple of blocks away and finding a parking space on the narrow street was nearly impossible.

Blinking multicolored Christmas lights ran up and down both sides of the city street between the lampposts, the same exact ones that had been there as I grew to adulthood and who knew how long before that.

The front door jangled as I opened it and stepped inside. *Jingle Bell Rock* was blasting from a small stereo that sat on the drugstore counter. Standing behind the register, the cashier was whistling to the jolly melody while reading a magazine. I walked to the cold/flu aisle and found what I wanted. After paying him, I stepped out onto the snow and ice covered sidewalk and waved, holding my hands out apologetically at a man wearing a Santa Claus suit who was shaking a bell for the Salvation Army, sorry I didn't have any change.

The main downtown area was three blocks long and to me, even feeling lousy, it looked wonderful. Christmas music drifted out of large speakers in the center of town, and I sang along with Bing Crosby's *White Christmas*. I walked along the sidewalk, stepping around people carrying shopping bags and those dressed up in dazzling clothes and headed to other engagements, feeling physically drained.

As I neared the historic section, back toward the studio, an antique shop caught my eye across the road. The shop was a remodeled Victorian row house, more like a tall narrow mansion, with an old-fashioned quality about the gingerbread eaves that made it seem like it had been there forever, yet I couldn't recall seeing it before now. That puzzled me because I knew I had done a lot of walking when I lived at home. Curious, I crossed the road and admired the large, black letters carved above an ornate wood door — RARE ANTIQUES. I got as far as the store's display window and stopped.

Lying on top of what appeared to be a carved

oak and brass hope chest was a pair of used gold pointe shoes with frayed white satin ribbons. Even if the shoes were the wrong size for Narissa, even if she wasn't advanced enough to dance on her toes, I knew they were perfect for her, the extra confidence builder I'd been hoping to find. The shoes glittered like spun gold. I had to have them. They could be an early Christmas present, I told myself. I couldn't pass them by

Glancing at my watch, I checked the time. It wasn't quite nine o'clock, so I pushed the door open and stepped inside. Antique clocks of various shapes and sizes covered the green plastered walls. Old-fashioned furniture of all kinds filled the store — finely carved woods polished with orange scented oil that permeated the entire room.

"Hello!" I called. No one answered. "Hello!" I called out louder.

This time someone did answer. "Hold your horses! I'm coming," an old man's voice snapped. Leaning sideways, I poked my head around an antique cherry wood dresser and spied a white haired man, with small round glasses perched on the tip of his nose. He was setting down an antique clock he'd obviously been tinkering with on a narrow workbench behind the counter. Tools of different shapes and sizes hung above the bench, tools that looked as old and well used as him. He turned, caught sight of me, and scowled fiercely, his face bunching into a mass of deep wrinkles.

"The store's closed!"

"Oh," I said, "the door was still open, so I walked in."

"I got busy and forgot to lock up." He shook his head and walked toward me like he was trying to catch a train. He pointed at a round brass clock on the wall, the face as big as the top of a barrel. "The store's closed!"

"The pointe shoes in the window! I'd like to buy them," I blurted out, ignoring his insistent hint to leave.

"Those shoes aren't for sale!" He kept walking, waving his hands like he intended to run me out of the store.

"No!" I reached out to him. "Those shoes have to be for sale! A little girl needs them!"

He must have sensed my desperation, because he dropped his hands. "Why?" He walked over to the window box, leaned over the chest and carefully picked up the shoes, cradling them as if he were holding a newborn baby. "Why these shoes?"

I pulled off my hat and shook some of the snow from my hair. How could I convince him that I needed those shoes? "Because I've never seen anything like them and because the little girl I'm buying them for is very special."

"How special is she?" He caressed the shoes like someone handling priceless gems. I could see the shoes meant a great deal to him.

"She has an arm that won't straighten, a deformed ankle, and the heart of a swan. She wants to be a ballerina." I paused to stare at the shoes and then at him. "And those shoes would make her VERY happy."

"I've had these shoes for a long, long time," he said to me. "They were my wife's, and she's gone now. Tell me more about your crooked swan."

I knew he was serious. Anyone who acted like he did as he fondled the shoes could be nothing less. So I told him Narissa's story. He listened attentively without saying a word. When I finished speaking, he kept staring at me as if he could see into my soul.

"So will you sell me the shoes?" I asked.

"No!" he said. "Please, leave."

Didn't this man have any feelings? "Why?" I reached out to him, begging with my hands, yet careful not to touch him so as not to offend in any way.

"Why, indeed," he paused.

Sensing immediately that he wanted me to say more, and knowing that if I said the wrong things the shoes would be lost to me forever, I took a moment to think. Why did I want these shoes? Was it only for Narissa? Or were the shoes for me as well? I closed my eyes, and I saw her face, heard her laughter, saw the sadness that enveloped her at times, watched her pirouette, trying so hard to dance like the others, and then it hit me. I knew what he wanted to hear because I could feel the rightness of it coursing through me. He wanted the simple truth. I could give him that.

I faced him squarely, felt our souls meet, and answered him. "Because I love her, she needs them in the worst way, and it would make me very happy to give them to her."

He held the shoes against his cheek and sighed, then closed his eyes and began to sway back and forth, humming a strange melody that raised the hair on my arms. I didn't dare say anything, so I waited. Thirty seconds passed…a minute…he continued to hum and sway, lost in another world, until I cleared my throat.

His eyes opened slowly. "Yes," he whispered like a man struggling to find his voice. "That will do. Tell her these shoes are magic!" And he placed the shoes in my hands. "Tell her anyone who wears these shoes becomes part of their magic."

Shaking, I swallowed a sudden urge to cry. "I'll tell her!" Worried that he might change his mind, I pulled my wallet out of my purse to pay him. "How much?"

Appearing insulted, the man backed away. "The shoes are priceless! They can never be bought!" He pointed at the door. "Now get out of here!" and he waved his hands like he was shooing chickens. "It's past my bedtime!"

I left that antique shop feeling warm all over, though the snowfall had increased considerably and it was much colder than it had been earlier. It seemed my feet sprouted wings, and I drove home humming Christmas songs that were playing on the radio.

Julie Helm

Ten

When Wednesday morning came, I was up at the crack of dawn, trying to come up with a plan to give Narissa the pointe shoes. At noon I called her home. Her mother answered the phone.

"Hello. I know we haven't met officially, but I've seen you at the studio picking up Narissa. My name is Kayla Davis. I'm Narissa's substitute dance teacher," I told her.

"I know who you are," said her mother. "Narissa has hardly spoken of anyone else."

"I hope it's all good," I joked good-naturedly.

"You've changed my daughter, Miss Kayla. There's so much I could tell you; Narissa's renewed enthusiasm for dancing has carried away many of the burdens she's had to bear."

"I need Narissa to come to the studio early today, before the other dancers in her class arrive," I blurted. "Can you help me?"

"Oh? Didn't Jan call you?" The concern in her mother's voice was unmistakable.

"No. I must have missed the call."

"Narrissa has caught a terrible cold. She talked me into going out with her last week after class to build snow angels."

Narissa was sick? "I really do need to speak with her before class. It's important," I told her, glancing at the Christmas gift wrapped with pink foil paper and tied with a wide green bow.

She sighed over the phone and my heart sank. "I'll ask her what she wants to do."

I'd take that. "Thank you," I told her.

We said our goodbyes and hung up.

I dismissed the students before Narissa's class ten minutes early, then quickly pulled my dad's oversized coat off the hook in the foyer where I'd hung it that morning and put it on; it was the only coat that had big enough pockets to play the game I wanted to play. Most of the dancers had gotten dressed and left with their mothers when Narissa walked into the studio, her mother trailing behind. I leaned against a wall in the foyer and waited for her. I felt bad the minute I saw her; she looked terrible. She obviously belonged at home in bed. Her cheeks seemed sunken, and I realized she had lost weight. Her eyes were puffy and tired-looking. Her mother held up a hand before I could say a word. Don't, she pleaded with me silently. "Narissa has come to dance this afternoon."

Narissa wore her leotard underneath her coat. Her hair had been combed in the ponytail I'd grown so accustomed to seeing. "I WANT to dance," Narissa said hoarsely.

For a moment I didn't know what to say or do. "Let me see if you're ready to dance," I finally said, and watched as Narissa took off her coat and hung it on a hook above the bench.

She faced me then, looking up with worried eyes and searching mine for approval. Determined to play the part, I placed my hands on my hips and made a slow circle around Narissa, shaking my head as if disappointed. I winked at her mother, hoping she'd understand what I was about to do. "I don't think she is quite ready," I told them. Her mother hesitated. I winked again, more exaggerated.

Catching on her mother said, "Oh! You might be right!"

Narissa gave me a bewildered expression. "But I am. Look at me!" She coughed, her chest raspy and tight, and then holding her arms midair, as if floating, she turned in a slow circle to show me her leotard.

"No!" I shook my head, giving Dad's coat pocket a couple of pats. "You haven't guessed what's in here, yet."

"What's in there?" She sounded confused.

I shrugged playful like, then scrunched up my face and tapped my chin, as if solving a puzzle. "Maybe you better look and see!"

Intrigued, Narissa stepped closer and opened my pocket; her eyes grew wide. "A present," she said softly, "for me?"

I nodded. "For you."

"But I...I didn't get you one."

"That's not important. You don't have to get everyone a present that gets you one. That's not what Christmas is about." I pulled the gift from my pocket and handed it to her. "From me to you. Merry Christmas, Narissa."

Narrisa glanced from me to her mother. "Go on," her mother encouraged, smiling, "open it."

That morning while wrapping her present, I had pictured Narissa opening it slowly with delicate hands, but she was a little girl, and she tore into that present like most children her age do — with gusto! "Pointe shoes!" she exclaimed seconds later.

"*Your* pointe shoes!" Choked with emotion I clasped my hands together, unable to hide my own enthusiasm.

"They're gold!" She ran her hands over them as if she were petting a baby kitten, soft and tender.

I reached out and began untying the satin laces. "Try them on! The man who gave them to me said they were magic. He said that when you wear them, you become part of their magic."

"But I can't dance on my toes!"

"It doesn't matter. You can still wear the shoes."

"For my solo?"

I hesitated. Could she wear them for her solo? No. Experience had taught me it would only make it more difficult for her to dance. "Not for the solo," I told her. "You're a little too young for that, yet. You need to develop your muscles, get stronger, and grow a little. But if you work hard, and you don't try to stand on your toes, you can wear them in class today. How's that?"

Her face lit up like she had just seen Santa Claus in the mall. She sat on the bench and immediately tried one on. It was too big. As she held her foot up for me to see, I pulled a large wad of cotton out of my other pocket and waved it in the air. "A dancer always comes prepared." She took off the pointe shoe and handed it to me. I stuffed the toe with cotton and had her try it on again. This time it fit—not perfectly, but better. The second shoe required less cotton because of the odd shape of her heel. When we had both ribbons wrapped around her feet and tied, Narissa stood and danced around the foyer. Though her movements seemed sluggish, and her chest sounded congested, her facial expression would have lit a starless night. She gave us a ballerina curtsy to complete her performance, stretching her arms as long as possible, and her mother and I clapped our hands and cheered.

The girls in Narissa's class began arriving, and I knew class should be starting soon. "I see a lot of improvement!" I said, thinking how lucky I was to be teaching her. "I'm very pleased."

Narissa hugged me. "Thank you, Miss Kayla. Thank you. Thank you."

"Do you feel like dancing today?" I asked her, allowing concern to edge my voice. "Or would you rather sit and watch?"

Narissa immediately frowned. "I want to dance!" she said to me. "I have the solo!" She turned to her mother, reaching out to tug on a sleeve.

"Yes, but Narrissa—" I began.

"I told her it would be okay," interrupted her mother.

"I can do it, Miss Kayla," Narissa assured me.

"Okay," I told her.

That afternoon the girls made a wonderful fuss over Narissa's pointe shoes. I told them the shoes were for Narissa, and that one day she would probably dance a solo in them. So Narissa wore them during class and seemed inspired; to my surprise she actually danced better and limped a little less. She shouldn't have been able to do it, but she'd been catching me off guard from the moment I met her. Her coughing slowed down, and even her congestion sounded better. All the dancers worked hard. There were still those times, due to Narissa's handicap, that her pirouettes were slower and not on beat. Even so, the others compensated by slowing down to wait for her. I was so very pleased with the progress being made. Jenny wasn't there again, and for that I felt bad, because a couple of the girls asked about her.

"Jenny has decided not to dance for a while," I told them. Then I got an idea. "But that doesn't mean you can't call and tell her how much you miss her. Invite her back to class," I told them. "Tell her the costumes Miss Sophie ordered have arrived. She's more than welcome to come and pick up hers."

"Yes, Miss Kayla. We'll tell her," they chimed one after the other.

I nodded, feeling better, then turned and walked briskly to the back wall where brown boxes that contained all the dancers' costumes were stacked and labeled. As I searched for the right box, I raised my voice above the chattering noise of the class and spoke over my shoulder, "Ladies, I know you're all excited to see your costumes, but please do not take them out of their individual packages. I want to make certain each of you gets home with your costume in one piece. With the help of your parents you need to be in full costume for our first dress rehearsal."

As I called out each of their names, the girls continued to talk and giggle.

"Oooh, earrings!" exclaimed Heather, who was the first girl to inspect her package, spying her jewelry clipped to a square piece of cardboard inside.

"We get to wear necklaces too?" said Adeline, watching Heather and jumping up and down. "I haven't got my costume yet, Miss Kayla."

Narissa's mouth formed a perfect "O" when she received her package. "Look, the dress is white with red velvet," she said looking right at me.

Her enthusiasm tickled me. They all made me laugh because I remembered a time when I had acted just like them. And though I was no longer an impatient little girl, I still got excited when receiving a new costume for a performance.

"Can't we please try on our costumes?" they all begged.

Though pleased, I shook my head. "Not until you get home. If there are costumes that don't fit right, your mothers will need to call Jan Stevens tomorrow so that alterations can be made. I don't want any of you wearing them before dress rehearsal."

Next Monday afternoon, Jenny and her mother walked into the studio shortly before class began. I was already on the dance floor when I noticed them, so I excused myself and walked to the foyer where the two of them waited for me. Jenny had taken her coat and boots off and was ready to dance.

"Jenny hasn't felt well the last couple of weeks," she explained. "But she's ready to participate today and…" She hesitated, apparently thinking, "we're sorry for any inconvenience we may have caused," she finished in a rush.

"Great!" I threw an arm around Jenny's shoulders and gave her a friendly…pat. It didn't really matter if one of the girls had called her, she was here and that's what counted. "Take a place at the barre," I told her.

Giving her mother an appreciative nod, I walked back out on the dance floor where the other dancers stood warming up. Nothing more was said, and I pounded my stick.

Narissa came in late wearing her pink ballet slippers and leotard, but she looked ill, paler than last week and without energy. She had a difficult time keeping up with the other dancers. Even the dancers slowing down didn't seem to help her. She coughed throughout the class, a dry tight cough that had me worried. The redhead and the blonde in pigtails tried to perk her up with words of encouragement, but she didn't seem to hear them. I grew concerned about the way I had been pushing her. She didn't complain; she just kept trying harder. Her improvement had been nothing less than remarkable, yet her health seemed to be going downhill.

After class, Narissa hurried off the floor. She was back seconds later, holding something behind her, acting as if she wanted to talk to me.

"What is it, Narissa?"

"I have something for you!" She handed me a colored picture that I knew immediately she had done herself. I took it from her and studied it. It was a self portrait: the picture was of a ponytailed little girl dressed in a pink, fluffy dance costume that hung past her knees. A smile spread slowly across my face when I noticed that instead of ballet slippers she had drawn gold pointe shoes on her feet. A large silhouette of a swan had been traced behind the girl.

"This is you!" I said, purposely raising my voice.

Narissa gave me a wide grin, like a child who has

just lost her first tooth.

"It's enchanting!" I told her. "You draw beautifully."

She clasped her hands together and laughed. "I knew you'd like it!"

Her voice was hoarse, yet her laughter thrilled me. She looked so pleased. "I don't just like it," I told her. "I love it!" And I bent and kissed her on both cheeks. "You're wonderful to do this for me!"

The sweetest expression crossed Narissa's face. "I love you," she said, and threw both of her arms around me and squeezed hard. I felt the warmth of Narissa's hug for the rest of the day.

I took the picture home that night and tacked it on the wall of my bedroom, right next to some framed dancing certificates my mother had hung for me years ago. Every time I looked at it, I heard Narissa laughing...

My mother came in later that evening to look at it. "So this is Narissa?" she finally said.

"Yes."

She placed an arm around my shoulder. "She's darling, isn't she?"

My heart swelled with pride. "She really is."

"I can't wait to see her dance," and she hugged me like she truly meant it.

Eleven

*I*sent home flyers on Wednesday letting parents know about the upcoming schedule: *There will be three dress rehearsals held at Stansbury Junior High inside the auditorium on Monday, Tuesday, and Wednesday from 6:30 to 9:00 P.M. Most classes will still be held on those days and NOT cancelled. The Christmas recital will be held on Friday, December 18th, seven o'clock at the same place. All dancers need to be there half an hour early in full costume. Hair needs to be pulled back in a ponytail or bun, with blue eye shadow, red lipstick, and blush on cheeks.*

That evening at the first dress rehearsal, I was busily passing out the remaining costumes when Narissa and her mother arrived. I had been secretly watching for Narissa, because I knew how excited she was about wearing her costume. When her mother saw me, she raised her hand, indicating, I assumed, that she wanted to talk to me. I turned to the dancers standing around me. "Start warming up on stage." I clapped my hands, sending them on their way, then walked over to Narissa and her mother.

"Narissa isn't feeling well," her mother explained when I came up to them. She glanced at her daughter. "She knows she's sick...but she insisted on coming."

113

I looked down at Narissa. Dark rings circled her eyes. She looked exhausted. "You don't have to dance today," I said, hoping the gentle understanding that she heard in my voice would convince her.

The frantic dismay Narissa suddenly expressed caught me off guard. "A soloist can't quit on the others. I want to dance my part. They need me!" she said hoarsely.

"You're sure? There will be two more dress rehearsals before the recital on Thursday, maybe you should go home and rest."

She shook her head. "I'll rest AFTER the rehearsal," she replied, and looked from her mother to me.

"Narissa —" I began.

"No!" she interrupted, again shaking her head.

Not knowing what else to say, I chanced a look at her mother.

Her mother gave me a helpless shrug and sighed. "Narissa and I have been arguing about this for over an hour now. She's promised me that she'll go straight to bed after the rehearsal. I'll be back in a little while to pick her up." She bent down and kissed Narissa on the forehead, sighed again, obviously unhappy about leaving her, and walked up the center aisle of the theater.

Narissa slipped her hand in mine as we watched her leave. When the theater doors closed, I felt Narissa turn to stare at me.

"You forgot about the swan," she said when I looked at her.

Narissa was right! It was her job to be the best that she could be. I should have known, even sick, she would give nothing less. "I won't forget again," I promised, and she appeared satisfied. I squeezed her hand and walked her to the stage. "Narissa," I said before walking away, "you look beautiful in your costume." She gave me the kind of smile that only she could give.

Rehearsal was difficult for Narissa. Even when the dancers tried to compensate for Narissa's awkward moments, it didn't seem to make a difference. The music was too fast and Narissa too slow. Her foot seemed stiffer, much more sore. She coughed and sneezed and repeatedly missed her cues. The stage lights seemed to bother her; she blinked and rubbed at her eyes. When she fell to her knees while straightening her back leg into an arabesque, then tried to stand, only to fall again, I finally asked her to sit and rest. "Watching a rehearsal is a necessary form of exercise, too," I told her, trying to make her feel better.

She didn't say anything. I could hear her taking short congested breaths—I imagined to keep from bursting into tears. Her eyes were watering, and I felt bad that I couldn't take the time to sit and talk with her more.

Sophie showed up shortly before rehearsal was over to show her students the new baby. Everyone ran from the stage. Narissa stood up and took a place in line, waiting for her turn to see the baby. The students were thrilled, Narissa especially so.

Narissa placed one of her fingers in the baby's tiny hand and glanced up at me, making a noticeable effort to keep her face away from the baby's. "He's so perfect!"

Sophie hugged her. "Thank you, Narissa."

Narissa and I stepped away to let others take their turn with the baby. She reached up and tugged me closer then leaned into my ear. "I want to be perfect," she whispered.

A lump rose in my throat, and I put my arm around her to show that I understood, that I wanted her to be as perfect as Sophie's baby, too. Pushing my pain aside, I traced a heart on her face and smiled. "I think you ARE perfect!"

She leaned against me. "I like who I am," she said loud enough for me to hear. "I didn't used to, but I do now. Even if I didn't have the gold pointe shoes, even if I didn't have the solo, I like being me."

"Narissa you are, without doubt, a very special

young lady." I stood with her sweet child's body against mine as long as I could, then lifted her in my arms and carried her to a seat in the middle of the auditorium where she could continue watching the other dancers practice on stage once the rehearsal resumed. My little swan had done enough limping for one day. I knew Sophie was watching, yet it didn't bother me.

Tuesday afternoon Narissa missed the dress rehearsal, and I hoped that she was home on an antibiotic and getting better rapidly. I gave the solo to Jenny and reminded her it was for rehearsal only. Jenny performed her moves precisely, yet I couldn't help feel that something was missing. As I stood watching her, I suddenly realized what was wrong. Jenny wasn't dancing from her heart; the mechanics were there, but the feeling was not. A picture of Narissa dancing formed in my mind. Six short weeks ago, I had asked for her heart and she had given it to me. I missed her.

Later that evening I called Narissa's home, but she had gone to bed, so I spoke to her mother. We discussed the weather, Sophie's new baby, the coming recital, and Narissa's failing health. Her mother sounded tired, but assured me Narissa was under a doctor's care and was taking an antibiotic, yet it seemed to me like she was holding back, and I felt obligated to say something about Narissa's solo.

"If you think the solo is too much for her, I could always replace her, give the—"

"No!" interrupted her mother, and I heard the naked fear in her voice. "Narissa is determined to see this thing through. It would break her heart if she couldn't dance now. She's been so happy. I can't tell you how happy. I'll make certain she rests more."

I knew I should make it easier for Narissa, and give the solo to Jenny. She could still dance but she'd have less to remember—but I couldn't bring myself to do it. Narissa had worked hard; she deserved to dance that solo. Who was I to tell her she couldn't? "Tell her I'll look forward to seeing her tomorrow in class and at the final dress rehearsal," I heard myself say. Struggling to keep my voice steady, I paused then added, "And that I love her."

"I'll tell her first thing in the morning," said her mother, forcing cheerfulness in her voice I knew she didn't feel. I felt uneasy, and yet I wondered if I was making more of Narissa's absence than I should.

Glad that I had at least tried, I said good-bye and hung up the phone. Sleep would be welcome tonight, and I rubbed my temples. Tomorrow would be another long day.

Narissa missed class on Wednesday and the final rehearsal that evening, which really concerned me. I called her home a few times, even left messages, but no one answered or called me back. I hoped that she was getting plenty of rest.

The Christmas recital was tomorrow. I had so many mixed emotions as I headed to Rosa's Bakery late Thursday afternoon to meet Sophie and David. They'd insisted on treating me to lunch to celebrate the occasion. I couldn't help feeling sad. Today marked the end of my days teaching for Sophie. I could hardly believe it was over. My thoughts turned to Narissa, how she'd missed class and the last two dress rehearsals, which still had me worried.

At the restaurant, I only ordered a side salad and water with lemon. I was still fighting off a cold and had no appetite. David spent most of the time telling me how much he appreciated what I had done, Sophie agreeing. Their praises went on and on. I spent my time pretending to listen to David and Sophie all the while thinking about Narissa. I excused myself from the table and went to the ladies room to try calling her one last time. Her line was busy, which relieved me some, but I was disappointed that I didn't get to talk to her. Her mother had surely listened to my messages. So why the silent treatment?

With Sophie recovering from the birth of her baby, I hadn't wanted to bother her, yet felt that I could no longer keep Narissa's absences to myself. I walked back to where Sophie and David were sitting and expressed my concerns. Sophie listened carefully. She kept brushing invisible crumbs off her sweater and pants and fidgeted in her seat until her feet began a constant tapping under the table, and I could tell that I'd gotten her concerned.

"Listen," she said when I was finished, "I know where Narissa lives. I'll stop by and check on her on the way home. If there are any problems, I'll call you."

"Thanks. You're a life saver."

We left after that.

Sophie didn't call.

Twelve

I walked into the junior high at ten minutes to six Friday night, dizzy from too much antihistamine, and a stomach full of butterflies. My parents had insisted on coming early to drive me. With all the stories I'd told them about Narissa these past weeks, I could hardly wait for them to see her perform. Somehow, I knew even sick, she would come. Her mother and father might not be happy about it, but she would be here.

Sophie and David hadn't gotten here yet, and this surprised me. I had reminded the dancers in their classes to be at the school and dressed by six thirty, and I expected them to start arriving any time. The props, the lights, the music, everything was ready. Sophie's students — my students, too — had worked hard for this night, and I realized more than ever how much I enjoyed teaching them.

Eight minutes to seven, Sophie and David still hadn't arrived; neither had Narissa or her mother. I was confused. The noisy hustle of nervous, excited dancers kept my head spinning. Mothers asked questions constantly. I tried to answer most of them; I'd certainly had enough training over the years. Still, the place seemed like the opening night of a New

York ballet, and I could have used Sophie's help.

Surprised, I noticed the man from the antique store sitting in the center aisle, near the stage. He wore a look on his face like a man lost in another time and place, and I wondered what he had on his mind. I'd seen that look before. I knew the pointe shoes weren't really magic, yet they had certainly added an extra spark of vitality to Narissa's life; she loved them so. I made a mental note to remember to thank him after the performance.

Five minutes after seven and still no one had seen Sophie or Narissa. The auditorium was full of friends, parents, and relatives waiting to see the young dancers perform. My mother and father waved at me from their seats; I knew they sensed my concern. I didn't want to let anyone down, especially my parents. If they didn't show up soon, I would have to start the Christmas recital without them. I told the stage crew and dancers to get ready as I pulled the cell phone out of my pocket and checked to see if I had any messages. My battery was dead. Closing my eyes momentarily I cursed under my breath. I'd forgotten to charge it last night.

Ten minutes later I stood in front of the audience and the Christmas recital began. The dancers were wonderful as number after number was performed. The first two soloists, Heather Tilitson and Becky Nelson, came out on the stage too early, but the audience was gracious and receptive. Parents clapped. Boys whistled. And grandparents pointed and cried. The recital seemed successful.

Time passed far more quickly than it had done during the rehearsals.

As the music started up and the second to the last dance began, I found Jenny. It was nearly eight thirty. As a professional I knew what had to be done.

"You dance the solo tonight," I told her. It hurt to give Narissa's solo to someone else, but I had held off longer than I should.

Jenny looked at me like I was crazy. "Why?"

I pulled a hand through my hair. Why? A good question, and Sophie Hepworth was going to answer it for me as soon as this recital was over and I could hunt her down. "Narissa isn't here, that's why!" I snapped.

She pulled a face. "Sometimes you're weird."

I wanted to shout, to scream, to cry in frustration. "You're absolutely right, Jenny, I AM SO WEIRD," and I patted her on the head.

The music ended and the audience started clapping. I stepped aside, allowing the dancers on stage to run off the floor. Then I saw Narissa, standing across the stage with the other dancers, waiting to go on. *That's why I was so weird,* I thought. *Narissa's here!* My heart thumped wildly and for a moment,

I couldn't move; she looked so beautiful. She was wearing the gold pointe shoes. *Why not?* I told myself. *She's earned it!* She simply sparkled with enthusiasm. She waved at me, and I felt guilty. I should have known she wouldn't let me down. I blew her a kiss and watched her reach up to catch it. Smiling, she blew it back. Though I couldn't put my finger on it, something seemed different about her.

I left the stage and hurried into the audience to find my seat before the music began. Glancing around momentarily, I happened to catch the eye of the old antique dealer. I couldn't help wondering if he had come to watch Narissa dance. Or did he have family, perhaps a grandson or granddaughter that was a student at Sophie's studio? He caught me staring and nodded. My heart flip-flopped and a smile spread across my face wider than the Cheshire Cat's. Thoughts of the old man were forgotten as the dancers ran out to take their places and the lights dimmed. The girls began dancing and I found myself smiling…they had given me such a hard time that first day in class, and now look at them…

Narissa came out seconds later and took her position more radiant than any other dancer. The spotlight found her, and her solo began. I sat entranced, unable to believe what I was seeing. Narissa came alive; she was awe-inspiring: her arms and legs moved in perfect time with the music. Her leaps and pirouettes brought surprised exclamations from those watching her. I'd never seen her dance more gracefully or full of confidence. She danced a flawless jeté, turned and whirled, and did another jeté. Her hands and body moved with the music as if it had been written for her alone. She continued to whirl in and out of the other dancers as if her feet no longer touched the floor.

After her solo, the final part of the dance began. Narissa appeared to be leading the others, her energy sparking them all. They pirouetted in perfect synchronization, forming a half-moon across the stage. Arms outstretched, their bodies dipped toward the earth and plucked at the sky; they moved like the angels they were meant to be. By the time the dance was over, and Narissa was poised in a deep arabesque, hands crossed in front of her, I was crying. The crowd started clapping and didn't stop. Perhaps, they too, realized what Narissa had accomplished. She had truly found her center. I wondered, then, if it had been my imagination, or if I had really seen Narissa dancing on her toes?

I saw my parents clapping and waved at them. Laughing, I pointed at Narissa and mouthed her name. Not only were the dancers given a standing ovation, they came back on stage twice. The audience threw roses at the girls. The old man from the antique store caught my eye, and then waved. I threw a kiss back for good measure. "Thank you," I mouthed at him. I could hardly wait to congratulate the dancers; I was so proud of them all.

I walked to the front of the auditorium and had all the dancers come back out on stage for the finale.

Narissa stood in the middle of the dancers, still dazzling, as she danced with the others until the music stopped and the finale was completed. The audience clapped again. Sophie was still nowhere to be seen, but it didn't matter, the evening had been magic. As the cheering and clapping died down, I thanked everyone for coming then asked the parents to give their sons and daughters a chance to change before collecting them.

A rose that someone from the audience had thrown was lying on the floor in front of me. I bent over and picked it up, thinking that I would present it to Narissa when I saw her. As I was making my way backstage, I bumped into Jan Stevens.

"I've been looking for you," she said. "A nurse who said she worked at the hospital asked me to give you this note. She said it was urgent."

I thanked her then opened the note and saw immediately it was from Sophie. It seemed she had tried calling earlier on my cell phone and had missed me. She wanted me to come to the Valley Regional Medical Center, second floor, room 201, as soon as I could get there. "Kayla," she had written on the last line. "I mean it! If you can sprout wings, fly!"

Hoping that Narissa would forgive me, I slipped the rose in my pocket and made my way over to my parents. We were on our way to the hospital in minutes. The only thing I could think of was that something had happened to David, or even worse, the baby. A good friend of mine in New York had lost a four-month-old daughter to Sudden Infant Death Syndrome a year ago. She was so heartbroken over it that she had quit dancing.

As the elevator doors opened on the second floor of the hospital, I saw Sophie and David standing outside a door down the hallway. Sophie was leaning against David, her head on his shoulder.

Heart racing, I made my way towards them. My parents followed. "Sophie!" I said when I was closer, and kept walking.

At the sound of my voice, Sophie turned to me. I could see that she had been crying. Her eyes were red and swollen. David's looked the same.

Cold dread raced through me. "What's wrong? Is it the baby?"

Sophie reached for me. Her hands were shaking and she acted odd, like she was offering me comfort. "It's Narissa," she said softly, a terrible sadness in her voice.

"Narissa's fine!"

Sophie shook her head. "No, Kayla. Narissa isn't

fine. She died of pneumonia this evening at seven o'clock; her immune system failed, and her body shut down. Her mother told us it happened real fast."

Taking a couple of steps back, I gave Sophie a disbelieving laugh and shook my head. "You couldn't mean Narissa." I glanced at my parents. "I saw her dance tonight. She sparkled like the star on our Christmas tree. She was wonderful!"

Sophie and David gave each other a puzzled look. When David shrugged, Sophie turned and took hold of my hand. She moved to the door, taking me with her, and knocked.

"Why didn't you call yesterday?" I whispered loud enough for her to hear. "I waited for your call..."

"David's prize bull got caught in some wire and cut up pretty bad. We were up all night with the vet. I'm so sorry," Sophie whispered back. "It took us a while to recover." Squeezing my hand, she leaned into me, asking without words for my understanding.

Narissa's mother opened the door. She had been crying. Cold, icy fingers of dread clawed at me, shattering my confidence, and I began shaking. Behind Narissa's mother stood a man I supposed was her father. Both parents looked heartbroken, pain and grief evident in their tear-streaked faces. Another older couple, both with white hair, stood nearby, holding each other close.

Her mother gave me a funeral smile, a forced expression of pleasantness, tears forming anew. "I'm so glad you've come. Please come in," she spoke in a quiet voice, and moved aside so we could enter. "Narissa made me promise to give you something." She stepped around a chair and was reaching for her purse on the floor when I saw Narissa's frail, still form lying on top of the bed, and I thought my heart would break.

Narissa's mother picked up my hand and placed something in it. "It was my grandmother's," I heard her say, "but Narissa insisted that you have it." Forcing myself to look down, I saw the crystal miniature of a ballerina. It was exquisite! So delicate.

I looked at Narissa's mother, her face full of gratitude, yet the harsh reality of her loss lining her face. "This was Narissa's way of thanking you for everything you did for her," she said and turned to where Narissa was lying. "She so loved to dance."

Bewildered, I walked over to Narissa's bed. Tucked under her arms were the pointe shoes I had given her, the satin ribbons entwined in her fingers. The gold in the shoes seemed to gleam brighter. Perhaps the shoes *were* magic. I thought briefly of the old man in the audience tonight.

"Narissa," I whispered. "How can I let go?" I stood there, staring, tears running unchecked down my cheeks, thinking of how Narissa had touched me. She had brought the joy of living back into my life and taught me more about courage and determination than I could learn dancing in a thousand ballets. She was my friend, and I would love her forever.

I pulled the rose from my pocket and laid it on her hands, knowing now was not the time to tell her mother that her daughter had indeed danced her solo at the Christmas recital, even after her death. She would find out soon enough, and there would be more tears. "For the swan..." I said instead, and closed my eyes. I saw her again as she stood and waved, blew me that last, sweet kiss just before going out on stage, and I knew she was happier than she had ever been. Wiping the tears from my cheeks, I whispered softly, "Dance for me in Paradise."

Julie Helm

Epilogue

*T*wo months later I stared in disbelief at the old clockmaker's shop with the gingerbread trim and black lettering that spelled RARE ANTIQUES above the door. A large FOR SALE sign had been taped against the front display window. How was that possible? It made absolutely no sense. What had happened since Christmas? Was this really the house Sophie asked me to check out last night? Suddenly I wasn't so certain. Sophie had said the place had two large floors besides the main floor and would be perfect for the partnership the two of us had in mind — a place where new students would be welcome because we had plenty of room for growth. Narissa's death had brought the realization that I didn't just *want* a change…I *needed* a change in my life. But I had no idea the house she called me so excited about was this one.

Standing there stupefied, winter rain splashed wet and sloppy on my face and hair and stayed there, making it hard to see after climbing from my new — but used — Ford Bronco. Sitting in the car had made me anxious. Getting out of the car allowed me to pace. The realtor was late! Had he forgotten he was meeting me here? I closed my eyes, instantly seeing Narissa's sweet face, waiting for the crushing pain I felt to ease. It was difficult at first because all I could see was her dancing...struggling to fit in...to move as well as the other dancers in her class...her face beaming with happiness when I told her the story about the swans. A few tears escaped and I reached up and wiped them away, knowing deep down that only time would heal this kind of hurt. Narissa would be a part of me now forever.

Yet doubt spiraled inside of me like hungry vultures. I wanted to believe that what I was doing was the right thing for me and everyone else. Change IS good, isn't it? Why then did it feel so scary? I could almost hear my mother saying, "Kayla dear, if nothing ever changed there'd be no butterflies in the world!" That had always been one of her favorite little sayings. I'm not even sure where she'd heard it...her mother? And so here I stood in the middle of a winter thaw freezing my feet off...worried sick and waiting for some insufferable realtor to show up. Taking a deep calming breath, I wiped away the icy splat of water that had landed in the center of my forehead, and opened my eyes.

The same large house I'd found the gold pointe shoes in weeks earlier still loomed in front of me. Twisting my lips in consternation, I wondered again about the FOR SALE sign in the window. There certainly hadn't been one when I'd found the pointe shoes. The tape on the sign looked brown with age. Before Christmas, a brass trunk had sat in the window. Inside there had been oak and cherry wood dressers, carved hall trees, coffee tables with clawed feet, multiple clocks hanging on the wall, and a lively old man with white hair and round glasses. I'd nicknamed him the clockmaker, because that's how I thought of him. What had happened in such a short period of time? I'd even seen him at the Christmas recital. He looked happy enough then. I had meant to find the time to thank him again after Narrisa's funeral.

Instead my parents and I had packed our bags and along with Sophie, David, and their two children had driven to Agate Mountain National Park for a much-needed New Year's trip.

After that, Sophie, David, and I had a few serious discussions that carried on late into the evenings about me possibly working with her at the studio. My parents added their advice and encouragement, and before long I was back to helping Sophie teach dance again. The camaraderie we had together at her studio worked; we meshed like a well-tuned piano. The dance contract I'd agreed to renew was given back unsigned, and the lead role in the upcoming ballet in New York permanently postponed. So the days flew by much faster than I anticipated, and the chance to thank the old man from the antique shop had come and gone.

So why then was I so bothered the old antique shop looked completely vacant? Perhaps because this old house represented something very real that had happened to me; the reality of it all had reached inside of me and awakened a sleeping heart...the clockmaker had been real...Narissa dancing in the pointe shoes had been real…the magic had been real, too, right? Was this really the place Sophie told me to check out? The address she gave me after she'd called the realtor was still in my purse. I'd shoved it in there before leaving the house this morning. Shaking my head I quickly pulled the paper from my purse and unfolded it. Yep. This was the place. So where was the realtor? He told me ten o'clock, and it was already ten thirty. Maybe he'd know the story behind the old man's sudden closure.

Fifteen minutes later, damp and chilled, my hair falling in wet chunks that only a blow dryer could fix, a man in a black Camaro pulled up to the curb behind my Bronco, spraying black street slush on me from my toes to the tops of my now frumpy hair, making me even wetter.

I immediately began brushing the dirt and ice from my coat and pants. "Crazy men drivers!" I mumbled under my breath. If I didn't want to know why the antique shop was closed so badly, I probably would have walked away right then…marched over to my Bronco, slid inside and driven off. I was preparing to say something, certain I'd regret it later, when he stepped out of the car…and I froze.

Please tell me this wasn't the realtor! Of course he wasn't, I assured myself—except the black-bearded handsome anesthetist from Sophie's birthing room now stood before me in the flesh. "You!" I managed to sputter.

"I'm so sorry! I had no idea the car would throw slush your way." He shut the door and walked toward me.

Fighting the sudden urge to pull a clip from my purse and tug my hair into a bun, I pointed at the antique store. "I'm waiting for a realtor. The jerk was supposed to be here to show me this house. He's late. And I'm already soaked to the bone. So don't worry about it. I certainly can't get much wetter." Was that his heart or mine beating so loudly?

He studied me momentarily with eyes bluer than a summer sky and sighed. "I'm that jerk," he finally said, offering me a smile that begged for a truce between us.

Did he just say he was the realtor? Was there a hole nearby I could hide my head in? "But you're the anesthetist. You gave Sophie her epidural." He lifted an eyebrow and gave me a smug sort of 'You remember me' grin.

"And part-time realtor, at least until I can pull more hours at the hospital. That's where I was just now. I'm afraid expectant mothers don't wait. I tried to call, but Sophie wasn't answering her cell, and she didn't give me your number." He looked from the house back to me. "A dance studio, huh?"

I couldn't believe I'd just called him a name like some angry schoolgirl. "Ah...yeah. I mean...I didn't know. Sorry I called you a jerk. I'm not usually like that."

He gave me another smile that had me curling my half-frozen toes. "Dayne Bradley," he told me holding out a hand, "realtor and anesthetist here to serve."

"Kayla Bradley," I replied without thinking. "No no no…uh, I meant Davis, Kayla Davis," and I reached out to shake his hand, unable to hold back my own grin. "Sorry." Something about this guy made it hard for me to concentrate. I hadn't been on a date in over a year. If he didn't ask me out, I decided right then I'd figure out a way to meet up with him again.

"It's okay." Dayne glanced again at the antique store and back at me. "You look like you're freezing to death. Let's go see what this place has to offer."

I nodded. Sophie had called the realtor last night, not me. She must have known all along who would be helping me. "Okay. Sure," I managed to say. She and my mom were two peas in a pod, weren't they? For some unexplainable reason I wasn't angry.

"I think a dance studio's a great idea. It's certainly big enough," he told me. "I haven't ever shown it, but I've been inside a couple of times. It's got three large floors and an oversized attic—quite the old place."

Dayne reached down to guide my elbow and together we walked to the door. "I was just here at Christmastime," I told him as he slid a key into the lock and turned it. "Was the old man who worked here the owner? He gave me a gift…"

The handsome anesthetist/part-time realtor was giving me a disbelieving look that was hard to ignore—one that oozed with doubt and a bit of amusement. "What?" I asked.

Dayne shrugged and pushed against the door, the rusted hinges creaking like squeaking ghosts, and he motioned for me to step inside ahead of him. "Take a look for yourself."

Panic thumped like a hammer inside of my chest. I didn't want to be sad any more. My senses were still reeling from Narissa's death. "He died, didn't he?" I swallowed hard. "Oh. I feel terrible. I wanted to thank him at the recital. He was there, too, that night. But it all got so hectic. Was it a heart attack?" I asked him in a voice shaking with regret.

Dayne still looked at me strangely. "Old age?" he answered gently. "Seriously…you need to see inside."

The shop was empty. Anyone could see that. I walked through the doorway like someone walking on thin ice. Dayne followed behind me silently. Our footsteps echoed in the hollowness that surrounded us. We stopped walking in the middle of the floor near the counter. Emotions rolling through me erupted, and I began to cry, sniffing miserably. The beautiful antiques were gone…no carved wood furniture from another century, no beautiful ticking clocks, nothing but peeling green paint and nails stuck in plastered walls...no old man with round glasses attempting to chase me out of the shop...nothing but a badly scratched hardwood floor and endless dust. Dust? Way too much dust! The place smelled musty with age and the lack of fresh air.

"Kayla?" Dayne's voice broke into my thoughts, bringing me back to the present. "You all right?"

My cheeks flushed bright crimson. I quickly looked away, my attention drawn once more to the deterioration of the old house. "Something's wrong," I told him frowning.

"You got that right." Dayne sounded relieved. "The shop has been closed for years."

"Years!" I exclaimed. "That's impossible! I was just here..." And yet, was it any more crazy than a little girl dancing like an angel at a Christmas recital hours after her death? "...I met him before Christmas, talked to him in THIS shop." I glanced around myself, dazed. "It was filled with rare antiques...such beautiful things..." I hiccupped but no longer cared what I looked or sounded like for that matter. "I can still see him. It was snowing that night. I was tired and sick...desperate for help. I walked into this very store and he helped me. He told me a wonderful story about his wife and gave me..." I stopped speaking, suddenly paralyzed by what I was seeing. Something WAS left in the store. An oblong box sat on top of the well-used workbench behind the counter. It was sienna brown and twice the size of an ordinary shoebox. Odd that it didn't appear to be covered in layers of ancient dust. "Oh my gosh!" I whispered.

"What?" Dayne whispered back, sensing he needed to keep his voice down for some unexplainable reason.

I nearly laughed out loud at the expression on his face. "No. Look!" I told him, and quickly walked over to the box. Running a wet glove over the top of it, I held my hand up for him to see what I had already noticed.

He appeared perplexed. "No dust?"

"Exactly! How long did you say it's been again?" I asked him.

Dayne looked about the place, more for himself than me. "A long while?"

Patterns of pink pointe shoes had faded into the brown cardboard on the box...patterns that defined dancing and the world I understood. "It couldn't be," I told myself as I carefully opened it and the smell of ballet rosin enveloped my senses. The box was packed to the brim with pointe shoes of all colors — pink, red, black, white, green, and the palest blue...all of them showing some amount of use. Silk ribbons wrapped carefully around each pair by loving hands...hands that knew whoever found these shoes would cherish them. "He left them for me," I whispered, nearly breathless with excitement. "And I know exactly what to do with them." I placed the slightly warped lid back on the box, carefully wiggling it back into place. How many Narissas were still out there? How many little girls searching for something to give them new meaning in life...how many who needed what I could give them...love...

"Who did?" Dayne asked, interrupting my thoughts.

Lightheaded and giddy with joy I turned to him, allowing every emotion flooding my senses to spread across my face. "The magic clockmaker, of course." And I picked the box up and twirled around and around. Dust billowed as sunlight burst through the front window, merging to form the nameless shapes of childlike dancers brought to life in prismatic sparkles suspended in the room for only a moment. "We'll take the house," I told him laughing in amazement. "It's perfect!"

About the Author

Julie Helm has always had a deep love for spinning fantastical yarns for the young and the old--anyone really, who was willing to listen. She grew up in Idaho Falls, Idaho and was raised by a single mother along with four other sisters. As a girl Julie also had a passion for dancing and took three years of ballet. In her first semester in college she took ballet and modern jazz until she injured her knee and could no longer pursue a career in dance.

Julie followed her husband abroad as they spent several years raising their family in Idaho, Tonga, Puerto Rico, and finally settling in Utah. She presently lives on a five-acre ranch in Utah with her city-slicker husband, who can ride a fox trotter like a seasoned cowpoke, her naughty Shih Tzu with an eating disorder, and five wild horses. Julie has six wonderful children and eighteen grandchildren. She enjoys science fiction and fantasy novels, taking her grandchildren rock hounding, and eating Junior Mints with popcorn at the movies. To contact her or schedule a signing, email her at julie@diamondgatepublishing.com, or visit her website at www.diamondgatepublishing.com.

Enjoy another book by Julie Helm

Merlin for Sherman

Sherman has officially gone off the deep end, or so he thinks, when he agrees to take a wild trip on a magic carpet into the unknown with a crazy old wizard named Merlin. The carpet hop scotches across the Earth and sets him down in a strange new land apparently countless years back in time. Sherman quickly finds himself hunkering down in tall ferns, dodging giant dragonflies, and struggling to make friends with the local dinosaurs. Oh my, what has Sherman gotten himself into?

Order your book today at

www.diamondgatepublishing.com

Enjoy another book by Julie Helm

The Lost Monster Tales

Monster in the Lake is a heart- stopping adventure that takes Brigham and his younger brother, Nick, for the swim of their lives. The bellowing and splashing of the lake monster they hook is nothing compared to the lesson they learn for disobeying their parents.

The Winter Fairies is a story for all those who aren't afraid to believe in a little fairy magic and the imaginative minds of Becca, and her sister, Amber. Come join the girls as they win the trust of winter fairies whose wings have been frozen in ice and who are desperately in need of their help.

Worm Hole is an enchanting story about Brianna and her brother, Steven's, quest to help a very fat green worm, who thinks she's a caterpillar—but really isn't—find a place where she belongs and friends who appreciate her. Discover with them the wonder of life and the satisfaction found in being unique.

Jared's Pet Snake is about a boy who wants what all boys his age dream about: a pet of his own. But Jared doesn't want just any pet—he wants a snake. To prove his sincerity, he's willing to do almost anything to get one. Unfortunately, the big, colorful, weird-looking snake Jared chooses at the pet store is far from ordinary. Jared and his mom discover one night just how remarkable!

The Night Something Nearly Ate Nannie is a delightful story about a Nannie who discovers a very hungry Bigfoot in her barn one night. Nannie's spine-tingling fight, to keep from being eaten, leads to a surprising discovery about the Bigfoot that everyone in the family will enjoy.

Order your book today at

www.diamondgatepublishing.com